UNFORGETTABLE

UNFORGETTABLE

FERN SMITH-BROWN

GoldenIsle Publishers, Inc.
2395 Hawkinsville Hwy

Copyright © 2000 by Fern Smith-Brown

This is a work of fiction. All of the characters in this book are fictitious, and any resemblance to actual persons, living or dead, is purely coincidental.

GoldenIsle Publishers, Inc.
2395 Hawkinsville Hwy
Eastman, GA 31023

Library of Congress Catalog Card Number: 99-96550

Fern Smith-Brown, 1939-
Unforgettable/Fern Smith-Brown

ISBN 0-9666721-6-X

1.Contemporary Romance—Maine—fiction. 2. Mystery
I. Title: Unforgettable.

Printed in the United States of America

First Edition

10 9 8 7 6 5 4 3 2

By the same author

Fiction

Plantation
The Talk Of The Town
Copper Kelly
What Made Sarah Cry
Whispering Winds
The Caballero Bandido

Non-Fiction

The Beckoning Hills-Chronicles of the Hamlet of
Darlington
Touch Me With Your Smile
Speak To Me Of Love
God Is On The Mountain

Children's Books

If I Could Be Anything - I'd Be A Fish
In A Child's Garden
Silly Rhymes From Father Moose

DEDICATION

To Grace Smith Trafton, Marian Smith Beals and Earl B. Smith, Jr. for an unforgettable summer on the coast of Maine and in loving memory of Aunt Alice and Uncle Earl who opened their hearts and home to make that summer so very special.

1

. . .like a plumed Knight

Ingersoll

*C*amilla Lloyd's small car swerved dangerously close to the soft shoulder of the road. She jerked the steering wheel to bring the red Corvette back to the center of the roadway, swiping angrily at the tears distorting her vision.

"Damn him!" she swore with a shake of her blond head, her small palm striking the steering wheel. "How dare he do this to me!" And a fresh flood of tears accompanied her words.

She sniffed audibly, wiping the vagrant tears that streamed down her cheeks with the back of her hand. She loved Branson so. It had never occurred to her that he might be cheating on her. How could she have been so blind -- so stupid, she berated, thinking back to all the dates he'd broken, all the late nights he claimed to be working. And still, she never suspected, always taking him at his word, always trusting him.

She remembered how her heart had thumped the first time she'd seen him. Eyes as blue as summer skies had met hers across the room of Janet Edwards' New Year's Eve party. He'd nodded his blond head, acknowledging her slow surveillance, and Camilla had felt a flush sweep over her features. With a distinct measure of difficulty, she dragged her gaze away, looking up as Charlie Marsh asked her to dance.

"Sure," she replied absently, pushing to her feet, while trying to ignore the blue eyes across the room that she knew were still watching her.

Charlie was only a casual acquaintance, someone she'd seen on occasion at other mutual gatherings.

"Tell me, Charlie," she ventured, above the loud beat of the music, "who's the hunk across the room, there by the piano?"

Charlie turned her adroitly, never missing a beat or step, to see who had captured her interest. "The blond guy?" he asked. "In the pin stripe suit?"

Executing a sharp pivot, he turned Camilla so that she could see across the room. Her green eyes swept over the tall, slim subject of their discussion. "Yes. Do you know him?"

"Not really. He's new at the medical center. Some kind of specialist."

"Aren't they all?" she murmured, running her fingers through golden blond hair that swung along her jaw line. The music stopped, leaving them at the far end of the long room.

"He came with Renee' Thomasen," Charlie was saying. "Want me to get her to introduce you?"

"Hardly," she said with a short laugh. "Nothing makes enemies faster than one woman showing interest in another woman's date."

Charlie laughed. "I get your point."

Janet approached, swooping down on them in her vivacious way. "Love your dress, Camilla." She circled round her friend, mentally appraising the short, pouf-skirted black dress that was a perfect foil for Camilla's blond hair and fair skin. Her smooth shoulders looked like porcelain, bare except for two tiny, silken spaghetti-straps that danced over one shoulder.

"Get this little number in Paris?" she cooed appreciatively.

Camilla nodded. "Actually, Daddy picked it out for me while he was there."

"Nothing too good for Daddy's little girl. He does spoil --" She stopped, wide-eyed. "Oh, God, Camilla," Janet muttered, remembering Camilla's father, Jonathan K. Lloyd, had suffered a heart attack and died en route from Europe less than six months ago. "I'm sorry. I wasn't thinking --" She put her arms around her friend, murmuring, "Forgive me."

Although she knew Janet's remark was unintentional, words of forgiveness still caught in her throat. Camilla could do little more than pat Janet's back in silent understanding.

Charlie took the awkward moment to sidle away.

"Janet," a pleasant voice interrupted, "introduce me to this lovely young thing."

Both women turned to the dazzling smile of Dr. Branson Phillips.

Camilla's eyes met his, and a smile spread across her features. He reached for her hand, not

3

letting it go, even after Janet had completed the introductions. From that moment on, they had become a couple. It had been a glorious year. Just two months ago, he'd proposed, and she had accepted his ring.

What had gone wrong? She thought they had both been happy, both looking forward to their future. Together.

Camilla's heart felt tortured when she relived the scene she'd encountered this afternoon. Painful as it was, the whole sordid scenario flitted through her mind's eye, scene by taunting scene. Having finished her meeting with her father's partner, she glanced at her watch. Impulsively she made the decision to stop by and see if Branson could join her for lunch. The meeting had gone much more quickly than she had expected. He would not have expected her to finish in such a short time. It would be a delightful surprise. They rarely had lunch together, his schedule being what it was.

At his office in a multi-storied building in Nashua's business district, she took the elevator to the fourth floor. Hurrying down the hall, her step was light, her heart happy, anxious to surprise him. She was sure he would be as pleased as she to have this impromptu luncheon together.

There was no receptionist at the front desk, so Camilla opened the door to his private office and peeked in. No Bran. She frowned, thinking she had missed him and that he had probably already joined some of his colleagues for lunch. Turning to go, she stepped back, pulling the door shut. Muted voices sounded from a small room off the main office. She paused. A giggle bubbled across the short expanse. It was one of those insipid, effected feminine giggles that grates over one's nerves. It

4

caused just such a reaction in Camilla and she paused, listening.

Another grating giggle. "You devil!" gushed the feminine voice.

A husky, masculine voice murmured sultrily, words that were spoken too softly for Camilla to hear. However, the woman's twittering echoed distinctly, and it scraped over Camilla's senses. There was no mistaking the indiscreet overtures coming from within.

Shock crashed through Camilla's delicate frame, and for the next few moments, she wasn't aware of her movements. She had no memory of crossing the room, didn't know that her footsteps had carried her soundlessly across the polished surface. Her hand had reached out of its own volition and pushed the inner door open.

The couple turned at the unexpected intrusion, staring in the same manner that Camilla stared at them. They tried frantically to straighten their disheveled clothing. The hasty movements knifed through her with such raw emotion that she felt like her own clothes had been ripped from her, exposing her very soul to the couple before her.

For one gripping moment Camilla's eyes closed, trying to regain her composure before meeting Branson's in one agonizing and heartbreaking glance. Unspeaking, she turned and retraced her steps across the room. Her fingers clawed at the third finger of her left hand, and as she passed the desk, she dropped the Tiffany style diamond ring onto it.

"Camilla! Wait!" She heard his voice calling to her, but she didn't stop. She ran down the hall, saw the elevator was busy and headed for the stairs, taking them at a neck-breaking pace.

Breathless by the time she reached the street, she paused only long enough to draw a deep breath of fresh air. Blindly, she crawled into the leather confines of the Corvette and then dissolved into tears.

Her happy, little surprise had exploded with devastating repercussions. It had brought her world crashing down, tearing asunder their lives and their future.

When she reached home, the phone was already jangling with a steady, unrelenting ring. The fact that it never ceased its incessant jangle told her it was Branson, and she ignored it. Like a robot, she moved with jerky, disoriented movements up the stairs to her bedroom, pulled a suitcase from the closet, and began stuffing clothes into it. While she packed, her mind was in chaos, and tears cascaded down her pale cheeks in tiny, glistening rivulets.

She had no desire to talk to Branson. Her heart was like lead. All she wanted was to get away. Away to some place quiet where she could think. Somewhere that he couldn't find her. It was over. She knew it. Her heart knew it. She didn't want to hear either his excuses or his lies.

A friend of hers, Claudia Moran, had a quiet little place near the coast in Portland, Maine. She knew she'd be welcome there. During a brief lapse in the ringing of the phone, she picked up the receiver in her bedroom and dialed Claudia's number, drumming the night stand impatiently with her fingertips. The unanswered ring echoed in her ear.

Camilla clapped the receiver down, caught a glance of her figure in the mirrored armoire doors. Her floral dress was topped by a dusty rose jacket. She gave her clothing only a cursory look, followed by a listless shrug, deciding to travel as she was. She had put a set of jeans and shirt in the suitcase. She would change after she arrived.

She picked up the suitcase and went back downstairs, confident Claudia would be home by the time she arrived.

The tears subsided in due course as she relived those horrible last minutes of discovering Branson's infidelity, giving vent to anger and disillusion. Mouth drawn in a firm line, she tried to quell the thoughts of the good times that were clamoring to be reviewed. Deliberately, she pushed them away, consigning them to oblivion. There was no point in recalling them. It would change nothing. Her relationship with Branson was over, dealt a severing blow by his own actions. Despite her brave convictions, her lower lip trembled, and her eyes threatened to spill over again. She tossed her head fiercely, refusing to allow them to flow.

She concentrated on the road that wound lazily along the shoreline, passing York Village and then Biddeford as well as other small, picturesque New England villages that dotted the coast.

At the Portland exit, she turned onto a secondary road that rose high above the ocean, overlooking Casco Bay. Ordinarily, the Maine coastline would have delighted her. She found beauty and charm in the little villages scattered along New England's coastal shores, as if tossed there, like so many lustrous pearls, by the unseen hand of the sea.

The white-capped waves that crashed against the gray rock shores were thunderous testimonies to the phenomenal mysteries of the deep blue sea. For centuries, artists had sought to depict them on canvas. Each one was different. Each one unique.

No artist ever captured the scene exactly the same. Today, however, with her heart and mind in havoc, Camilla paid little attention to it.

On the outskirts of Portland, she passed a Renaissance Faire but gave it only a cursory glance. With care, she threaded her way down the narrow street, past cars parked on both sides of the road. It had begun to rain, as though echoing the teardrops in her heart. People spilled from the carnival grounds, hurrying to their vehicles. A group of gypsy children, black hair flying in the wind, darted across the road in front of her. Camilla brought the car to a screeching halt.

With a slow shake of her head, she edged the car onward, turning up the speed of the windshield wipers. Fat raindrops splashed onto the windshield and over the roof of the car, bursting with a melodious tap - tap - tap.

Beyond the carnival site, she eased off the main highway onto a side road, driving slowly, peering through the rain-swept window for the sign that marked Claudia's drive.

Distorted by the heavy rainfall, and fuzzy to her vision, she finally saw the green and white marker with the name Cromwell. The rain showed no sign of lessening as she made the left hand turn onto the private drive. A short distance beyond, she spotted Claudia's small cottage. Her heart gave a little flutter for there was no sign of activity. She stopped the car, surveying the unlit house. Even the garage was shut up tight.

Camilla got out slowly, leaped over a puddle that had gathered in the driveway, and ran up to the porch. There was no answer to the buzz of the doorbell, and no evidence that Claudia was in residence. Camilla ran back to the car. Her jacket was soaked by this time, and she pulled it off, laying it across the back of the passenger seat. She started the car, planning to return to Portland and check into a motel. The car sputtered, caught, then sputtered again.

"Don't do this to me," Camilla begged frantically.

She tried to start the car again, but it coughed like a diseased body, and died. Camilla was horrified. Tree branches dipped toward her like beastly tentacles, threatening to consume her, car and all. The sky was black, lit up only when lightning streaked across its surface, appearing hell-bent on ripping it apart. And the rain poured with a vengeance. Slowly, she counted to five before trying to start the car once again. Her right hand turned the key, and her lips moved in silent prayer. Still, nothing. Her heart sank.

She thumped the steering wheel with the heel of her hand. A frustrated, "Damn it," bubbled past her lips, mingled with the fear in her eyes and the frustration in her soul. Accompanying it all was the storm outside that echoed the rage in her heart.

She sat there for a few minutes listening to the rain pelting the roof of the car. Resignedly, she knew she couldn't just sit there. She had to find help. In the back of her mind lay a nagging torment that pushed its way to the forefront of her thoughts. No one knew where she was. If she needed help, no one would come. Not one person knew of her intent to flee to Maine. No one would know where to find her. It would seem that she had simply disappeared. Vanished. Her heart thumped, and tears filled her eyes. Except Claudia, there were no close friends. Daddy was gone. There was nobody to care anymore. Not Branson -- especially not

Branson. Absolutely no one. She was rocked by
the admission that not only was there no one who
knew of her whereabouts, but also that there was
no one who cared. The melancholy thought brought
the tears streaming down her cheeks in a moment of
self-pity.

Then she jerked the door handle in sudden
anger. No need to sit here. "If I'm going to get out
of this mess," she muttered, "I'll have to do it on
my own." Surely, there would be a house
somewhere off the main road where she could use a
phone and hire a mechanic.

She gave one swift glance at her already wet
jacket and shrugged. It would do little good. In
seconds, she'd be soaked to the skin anyway. So
thinking, she pushed open the door, flung the strap
of her purse over her shoulder, and got out of the
car. Lightning struck again, very close, and with a
small scream, she leaped back into the car.

A long minute dragged by while she
gathered her courage around her like a cocoon.
Slowly, she opened the door and edged her way out.
Slamming the car door, she started running up the
dirt lane, her high heels sinking into the mud with
every step.

Thunder and lightning was now playing
havoc in the heavens. At the end of Cromwell
Road, beyond her, she saw a Dead End sign
wavering on the roadside, which she had not noticed
before. She hurried back up the road the way she'd
come. A dirt road crawled out of the woods into her
distorted vision, and she swung into it, praying there
would be a house at its end.

Rain poured in torrents. Trees on the
overgrown roadside bent with maddening force.
Leaves and branches literally covered the dirt road.

Thunder boomed, rolling across the heavens with a deafening sound and lightning flashed in a jagged streak. Camilla stood stock still amid it all, covering her ears with her hands and shutting her eyes tightly.

When the blinding light receded, she started forward again, then stopped. Had she heard a horse's hooves? She gave a little laugh, chastising herself. It was bad enough to be lost and stranded, but was she hearing things as well? She hastened her step, running and leaping over the fallen debris that lay in her path.

Just as she neared the bend in the road, the sound of hooves striking sodden earth was definitely audible. Camilla stopped, peering through the mist and driving rain.

At that moment, nearby thunder billowed like a drum roll, and a streak of lightning zigzagged across the darkened sky. It struck a tree on the roadside, and a limb splintered from the trunk. It dropped heavily, sailing toward earth, directly above Camilla standing awe-struck in its path.

When the heavens lit up, it showered an effervescent beam of light on the figure on horseback that was bearing down on her. Dear God! She was not only hearing things; she was seeing things as well. The thought streaked through her brain, emblazing it on her mind as indelibly as the lightning that stood out in bas-relief in the sky, for the tall figure astride the black stallion was straight out of King Arthur's Court.

Had she somehow crossed an invisible line into another dimension? She didn't have much time to ponder that, for he rode straight toward her, his eyes shielded, and his black cloak streaming out all around him. His mouth was opened, and he yelled above the din of the storm for her to get out of the way. But it was too late. Her last conscious thought was of the dark Knight thundering toward her on the back of an enormous black steed. The limb struck her in its descent, and Camilla crumpled to the ground in a sodden, limp heap barely visible among the leafy branches.

The tall cloaked figure dismounted and ran forward. Hard muscles rippled beneath the folds of the cloak as he pulled at the tree limb, tossing it aside. Swiftly, he bent to the slender figure that appeared not only lifeless but as pale as the silver-blond hair that lay plastered to her head. A horrible gash on her temple was bleeding profusely, mingling with streaming rain. Feeling for a pulse, strong fingers searched the slender white neck. There was still life in the frail form, and the rider lifted her gently into his arms, cradling her against him, though it was quite useless to shelter her from the storm at this point.

Clinging to his burden, he climbed astride the black stallion, spurred it gently, and rode away into the obscure blackness of the lane until that dense darkness engulfed him.

2

Habitant of castle gray.
Channing

*T*he gray stone castle stood stark and
menacing in the half light, crouched on its perch
overlooking the bay. Long abandoned, a dark,
cloying atmosphere surrounded it in daylight, and
with approaching dusk it was even more formidable;
ghostly in the rain and fog that was beginning to
hover all around, like spectral beings.

When Camilla awoke, her head ached
abominably, and her brain was fuzzy. Holding her
head very still, her eyes swung round the room. A
fire burned in a huge fireplace on one long wall.
Two enormous stone carved gargoyles, one on each
side of the hearth, supported the massive marble
mantle. Her eyes moved, hearing static and
someone asking for Galileo.

Painfully, she turned her head toward the voice, hearing it demand, "Galileo, are you there?"

In the dimly lit room, she saw a shadowy figure emerge from the dusky interior, draped in a dark cloak thrown casually around broad shoulders.

She saw him pick up a small hand device from the desk and speak softly into it. "Yes. I am here."

"Received your message about Goldilocks. Is she still there?"

"Yes." The reply was quiet.

A heavy pause preceded the next words of the voice. "It is impossible to put this mission on hold."

"I know."

"Then get her out of there!" said the firm voice on the other end.

"I can't."

"What do you mean, you can't?" demanded the voice authoritatively.

"She's been injured. She's still asleep."

"Well, get rid of her as soon as possible before she blows your cover."

"Would you just stay calm?" the dark figure soothed the troubled voice. "I'll handle this."

There was a very long pause before the voice said, "I don't have to remind you, we have a lot at stake here."

"I know. Don't worry. Nothing will go wrong with our plan. I have to go -- before she wakens."

The line went dead and the crackling static ceased.

A small fear rose in Camilla's breast. At the same time she was very aware that she didn't know exactly what she feared. Was it the dark stranger or the fact that while lying there listening to the cloaked figure, her nervous fingers had encountered the gauze wrapped round her forehead? A large patch was raised over her temple, and she suddenly realized that she did not recognize her surroundings, nor did she know who she was, or where she was. She felt a moment's panic but assured herself memory loss was due to the head wound, and she wondered how she had gotten it. She closed her eyes, trying to recall something familiar. Anything. But nothing came to her. Not so much as a flicker of familiarity. It was a scary feeling.

When she opened her eyes again, they encountered the cloaked figure. He was peering down at her from eyes as blue as midnight. She cowered beneath the blanket, her eyes not leaving the handsome, chiseled features. At the same time, she was intensely aware of the strong frame attired in Renaissance clothing. She didn't know why it seemed out of place, but it did.

"Don't be afraid," he said gently in a deep, mellifluous voice.

"Who . . .who are you?" she whispered over dry lips. "Do I know you?" She seemed to have some vague recall about the blue eyes and with that memory there came a sudden wash of sadness that engulfed her. A strange flutter began in her heart. Coinciding with that feeling of sadness was another inner sense that was telling her these deep blue eyes were different. She didn't know exactly what these senses were intimating, only that she should trust them. She was conscious of the fact that there was something different about the deep indigo eyes that looked down on her from the blue eyes in her memory that were making her heart ache.

His deep voice, responding to her question, interrupted her thoughts. "No. We've never met before."

"Then what am I doing here?"

"We're having a rather ferocious thunderstorm." He indicated the rain pelting the long window that she had not noticed until now. "A falling limb struck you. I brought you here and bandaged the wound for you."

"Thank you." The words seemed inane, but she couldn't think of anything else to say to him.

He smiled. Indulgently, but a nice smile. One that made little crinkles at the outside corners of his eyes.

"What is your name?"

She shook her head in a desolate little gesture, her brow furrowed. "I don't know."

It was such a woeful, sad response that he said quickly, "You took a pretty good whack on the head. Your memory will come back."

"Do you think so?" Again that little-girl-lost, seeking-assurance voice.

"Sure. It's only temporary."

He sounded so convincing, she asked, "Are you a doctor?"

A chuckle rumbled from his broad chest. "No. Far from it. But," he continued, "I think I should get you to one as soon as you feel able and . . . after this rain slows down."

But she was already shaking her head. "No. I don't want to go."

"You've lost your memory," he said gently. "It could be serious. You may even need to be in the hospital."

"No, please," she interrupted. "I . . . I just need some time. Please, don't send me away yet.

Let me try to remember, to . . . to find myself." Her eyes filled with tears.

And against his better judgement, he assured her quickly, "All right, we'll wait until tomorrow." His penetrating eyes flowed over her. "Do you remember anything? Where you came from . . . where you were going?"

She shook her head in that same desolate manner, pushing to a sitting position. In doing so, she moved the covers away from her body. Her eyes grew wide in shock.

Her legs were bare, and she was suddenly aware that she had nothing on but a shirt. It was of fine, soft linen, with a cascading flow of ruffles at the throat, and long sleeves that ended with the same froth of ruffles that nearly obscured her small hands. Did she detect the faint aroma of aftershave? Again, her senses were telling her this -- this poet shirt -- did not belong to her.

She swallowed. "My clothes. This . . . this is not my shirt. What have you --" Alarm made her green eyes luminous in the glow of the firelight.

He bent toward her.

She shrank back.

Immediately, he straightened, saying sternly, "Stop looking so frightened. It has never been necessary for me to take advantage of an unconscious woman." He glowered at her. "I simply removed your clothing -- "

"*You* removed my clothing?" she squeaked, a pink tint feathering across her pallid features.

"You were soaked to the skin. I had no other choice. You could have gotten pneumonia."

Camilla's eyes darted around the room. She couldn't hold his dark-eyed gaze any longer. It was humiliating. "Where are my clothes?" she whispered over restricting throat muscles.

"I sent them out to be laundered. They'll be back tomorrow."

Keeping her sight averted by focusing on the rain running down the narrow window panes, Camilla sought to steer the conversation away from her clothing -- or lack thereof -- to center on the stalwart figure towering over her. Some inner sense told her his attire was out of place. Yet, the room, the long narrow windows, the enormous dimensions of the fireplace echoed another age, all of which made him fit neatly into his surroundings. It was she who seemed to be peculiarly out of place.

She was overcome with the feeling she teetered on the brink between a century long past and a newer world in which she had no memory. Instead of trusting her senses, she asked, "Are you a Knight or something?"

"At the moment."

Forgetting her earlier embarrassment, Camilla swung her glance up to his face. "What does that mean?"

"I think you should be resting," he replied, giving her no explanation.

"I'm not tired." Her voice had the quarrelsome tones of an ill or overwrought child.

"Perhaps you're hungry? I have some soup. Let me get you some." Without giving her a chance to refuse his offer, he left the room, pulling the cloak from around his shoulders and tossing it over a chair.

Camilla's mouth drew up at the corner. God knows what kind of soup he'd bring her. She studied the room from its cold, marbled floor to the enormous height of the ceiling. A multi-branched chandelier swung from six tarnished chains, and she could see the stubs of candles in several of the numerous holders. She was definitely in a castle. How did she know that? Some tiny mind-controlling gremlin flung the question at her. Perhaps she wasn't in a time warp at all and did, indeed, belong here in this age that seemed so foreign. She shook off the feeling, coming back to cast another wary glance at the ill-kept castle. A small shudder went through her. The soup she was about to be served was probably going to be ox-head soup, or a dingy-colored liquid. Gruel came to mind, and she searched her dead brain cells for a definition.

The Knight returned carrying a tray with a small bowl and mug, their contents steaming. She almost hated to look at the contents. Yet, he really was trying very hard to make her comfortable. How could she refuse his kind offering? Camilla steeled herself. Be damned! She'd eat it even if it killed her! Unless, she thought upon reflection, it had something quite horrible floating in it.

The Knight set the tray on a small stand, leaned down to ease her into a more comfortable sitting position and to fluff the extra pillow behind her shoulders. He lifted her slim form almost effortlessly.

"Okay?" he asked, stepping back.

"Yes. Thank you very much," she murmured, pushing up the flowing sleeves that wanted to slip down over her hands.

Lifting the tray, the Knight carried it over to her and set it on her lap. He stood with arms folded, waiting for her to partake of his offering -- or perhaps to see to it that she did.

Stifling a cringe, Camilla glanced down. Surprise raced across her features, and she grabbed up the spoon, stirring it through the liquid. "Chicken soup?" she chortled unbelieving.

He nodded, then as if cognizant of her earlier presumptions, he countered, "What did you expect?" A black eyebrow arced in mockery.

"I . . . I -- " She sipped the broth delicately. "It's wonderful," she stated, scooping up another spoonful, then much to her delight, discovered that the thick mug held steaming cocoa.

Camilla watched him pensively over the rim of the mug. "Would you tell me your name?" she asked quietly.

"Dak."

"Dak?"

He nodded.

Camilla frowned. She may have lost her memory and not have any recollections of her life before he carried her here, but after she had regained consciousness, she distinctly recalled the voice on the statical radio asking for someone named Galileo. He had responded to it, speaking in low tones, assuming she was still asleep. She wondered why he would lie about his name.

She studied him. He was handsome, with a slender, athletic build. Yet, handsome wasn't quite the way to describe him. Distinguished seemed a more fitting word. Perhaps it was the gray wings that feathered across his temples that gave him that appearance. His dark hair was brushed backward, off his forehead. It looked like it had a tendency to wave, and he strived to keep it tempered into a more dignified and smoother look. His face was lean and tanned, his jaw chiseled. In the strong chin, she detected a bit of stubbornness. She liked his looks and guessed his age was about thirty. All in all, he was the perfect man, the kind that could look as well in a three-piece suit as he did in a casual pullover and jeans.

Camilla's eyes flickered, suddenly growing wide. Jeans! They didn't wear jeans in King Arthur's Court! They were fashion statements of the twentieth century. She felt pleased with her discovery, which told her in which time era she belonged. But then her frown deepened. How could she then be back hundreds of years in this castle?

"What is the matter?"' His voice interrupted her thoughts with its depth and sincerity.

She looked up.

"Is something wrong?" He moved toward the bed. "Or have you remembered something?"

"Jeans." It was softly spoken, solemn.

"I beg your pardon?"

"Jeans," she repeated, then added, "You wouldn't understand."

"Try me," he replied softly.

"Well," she began as though explaining to a child. "You see, where I come from . . . that is, the century I lived in, we wear jeans."

"And where is that?"'

"I don't know. But our clothes are completely different from yours." She waved a hand to indicate his attire. "In fact," a memory was dancing in her brain, "I packed a pair along with a pullover sweater in my suitcase."

"Suitcase?"

"Yes. Yes." Her voice was excited. "I had a suitcase. I remember that."

"Where were you going?"

She shook her head. "I don't know."

He touched her blond hair gently. "Don't worry. It will come back."

She reached up and caught his hand -- a strong hand -- before he could withdraw. "Please. Tell me. Where am I?"

He looked down on her upturned face, wondering at the urgency of her words. "You're in Portland, Maine."

Puzzlement drew her brows together. "Are you sure?"

"Very sure."

"But the cloak, your clothes . . . you're not from the twentieth century -- "

She heard him draw a deep breath before he plunked himself down on the bed. She had to scoot her legs over quickly to avoid having him sit on them.

He leaned over the tray to stroke her face. "You poor kid," he murmured. "I am sorry. I was not trying to deceive or confuse you. I carried you here out of the storm after you were struck by a falling limb. Obviously, you're suffering from amnesia -- and you're memory will, no doubt, come back soon. But," he said emphatically, "you are not in another century."

"I'm not?"

He shook his head. "No."

"But your clothes."

"I am competing in a jousting tournament at the Renaissance Faire on the outskirts of town. We wear the costumes for the benefit of the onlookers who come to watch the practice sessions. It adds a little color to the occasion. I was en route home when I heard you scream and came to investigate. You were struck just as I rode up. I yelled at you to get out of the way, but it was too late."

"But this place . . . this castle. It is a castle, isn't it?"

"It is. Derelict though it may be." His gaze roved over the interior, and he gave her a rundown on the history of the relic of a castle.

Built in 1870, Claire Castle had been built as testimony of Edgar Hedgeworth's love for a young village girl. The gentleman, of social prominence, was many years her senior, but the determined old fellow, smitten with adoration, promised to build the beautiful girl a castle if she would marry him. In time, she consented, and the castle was built of huge blocks of New England granite and constructed on a level site overlooking the bay with all its inlets and coves. Upon its completion, the couple were married with much fanfare. However, Edgar's happiness was short-lived, for his young bride soon fell in love with the gardener. One evening, in the dark of night, she ran off with her lover and was never heard from again. Edgar Wedgeworth fired his entire staff, closed all the rooms, and lived the remainder of his life like a hermit, using only one room of the huge mansion. After he died, the unkept castle fell into disrepair. Many years ago, one wing had been burned out by a careless vagrant in search of a winter's shelter.

The locals called it Claire Castle after the young girl for whom it was built. It had long since ceased to be of interest to the villagers, although whispers still lingered that the castle was haunted by old Edgar, pining and waiting for his love to return. The remains of the castle stood in ghostly shadow high on the bluff, abandoned for more than fifty years.

When he finished, she asked, "Is this your home?"

He hesitated, then shook his head from side to side. "No," he answered quietly.

The rambling castle was not the sort of place a single man would rent, and Camilla knew there was more to it than he was willing to say. Afraid to probe, she asked, "Is your name really Dak?"

Again the dark head nodded. "My friends call me Dak. It's short for Dakody. Dakody Brewster."

Still her brow furrowed. "Then who is Galileo?" she blurted.

Quickly, he masked the surprise at her question. "What do you know about Galileo?" he countered.

"Nothing. I heard it over your radio when I awoke."

"Oh."

She waited for him to go on, but he didn't, and so she repeated her question. "Who is Galileo?"

"I'm not free to answer that."

The frown deepened.

"What?" he asked, tracing a line on her forehead with his fingertip. "Is there something else?"

She hesitated, looking up to meet his blue gaze. "Goldilocks. Is that me?" she asked, her voice almost a whisper.

He smiled. "That's you."

He rose, sensing she was about to ask more questions. Questions he was not at liberty to answer. "You should rest." He lifted the tray from her lap. "The storm should end tonight. Tomorrow we'll try to find out who you are and where you're from and get you back home again." He strode across the room, balancing the tray.

"Dak?" Her voice was small, timid.

He turned back, waiting for her to speak.

Shyly, she said, "It's obvious this room is

your entire living area." She hesitated, stirring uncomfortably in the bed. "Where will you sleep?"

He strode out of the room without answering her.

Damn. Now I've made him mad, she thought. She must have sounded like some ninny who didn't have sense enough to trust the one person who had shown her nothing but kindness and had been the epitome of politeness. She heard him re-enter the room and peeped over her drawn-up knees at him.

He strode across the room, plunked down on the bed again and said, "Let's get something straight, Goldilocks. I told you before; it has never been necessary for me to take advantage of a woman conscious or otherwise. That's not my style. I am offended that you look at me and even *think* that I might do so." He glowered at her fiercely.

When he paused for breath, Camilla broke in to stem the provoked tirade. "I apologize. I honestly didn't mean for my words to sound so callous. It . . . it is apparent this is the only bed and, and -- " She stopped, floundering. "Okay," she admitted. "Maybe I am a bit uneasy. But it's not your fault. You've been very kind." She blinked her eyes, and the lower lip started to tremble. "It's just that I'm so confused, and I feel so helpless . . . so vulnerable that it scares me."

She sniffed. "What if I never remember who I am? And suppose no one is looking for me. Suppose there isn't anybody." She looked up at him with stricken green eyes. "Suppose I'm all alone with no one to care that I'm lost and --" Her words dissolved into gulps, and the green eyes spilled over. Her face crumbled and the tears began.

Dak reached for her. Oh, hell. Now he'd

gone and made her cry.

He didn't know how it happened. But the next thing he knew he had pulled her out from under the covers and scooped her onto his lap. He held her close to him, rocking back and forth. His head came down, leaning against her golden crown, and his lips crooned into her ear, "There, there Goldilocks. I'm sure there's lots of people who care. We'll find your family. Please don't cry. Come on, baby. Everything will be all right tomorrow."

He continued to hold her, letting her cry out her frustrations, while he whispered soothing words all the while. He could feel her tears soaking through the light fabric of his shirt to his bare chest underneath. Once, unconsciously, his lips brushed her temple in the middle of his rambling words of consolation.

Finally, the weeping subsided. She peered up at him, wiping at the vagrant tears with the ruffle of the sleeve of the poet shirt. "I'm sorry," she managed.

He smiled. "It's okay," he said softly, rising with her still in his arms. Her bare legs dangled over his arm, and she was thankful the shirt was long enough to cover her bottom. Bending, he nudged the covers back with his fingertips before setting her back in the bed. He tucked her legs beneath the covers, then pulled the warm folds up to her breast. Still bending over her, he brushed back her hair from her forehead, being careful of the broad bandage. "Okay?"

She nodded.

"Try to rest. I've a sleeping bag I'll throw down over there." He indicated the far side of the room, near the fireplace. "Don't hesitate to call

26

me. And please . . . don't be afraid."

He turned to go.

"Dak?"

He looked back.

Camilla held out her hand. He took it. Their eyes met, and she said, "Thank you. For everything."

He winked. "Go to sleep, Goldilocks."

She smiled and gave his hand a little squeeze.

3

. . . stand in the window of a castle.

Lucretius

Camilla lay staring up into the darkness.
Dak had crawled into the sleeping bag sometime
ago. She could hear his even breathing and knew
he was already asleep. The firelight flickered,
casting dancing light into the room. She could hear
the storm outside, and the wind crying to get in.
Everything was quiet and strange. But she felt
safe. She lay there a long time, her mind jumping
from one thought to another. Finally, she pushed
back the covers and sat up, her bare legs dangling
off the bed.

She looked over to the corner where Dak lay
unmoving in the sleeping bag. The stillness of the
room threw back his quiet breathing. It mingled
with the intermittent crackling of the wood in the
fireplace. Moving slowly and silently, so as not to
disturb him, she rose and padded barefoot to the

long, narrow window. She stood there looking out into the rain-filled night.

A sense of loneliness engulfed her, and unconsciously, she folded her arms around her bosom, cradling her body as though to take comfort from it. She lifted her head to gaze up into the bleak darkness of the sky. A shiver crept over her, and she went back to bed, pulling the covers up to her chin.

She could not know that Dak's ears had been trained to detect the slightest sound. Or that he watched her as she stood forlornly at the window gazing out with frightening and chaotic doubts about her future. The uncertainty emanated from her small personage, electrifying the air and creating dismal vibes that Dak was hard pressed to ignore. Despite the desolate image, he was intensely aware of another aspect of the small figure wrapped in the white poet shirt that enveloped her like a diaphanous cocoon. He saw a willow-slim sprite with a crown of golden hair that floated gently with every move. He saw the long, shapely legs, bare and seductive, with the firelight casting playful shadows over them. And his heart took a curious dip for he had noticed something else besides her beauty and womanly attributes. He saw the vulnerability she had spoken of earlier. It made him want to go and take her into his arms again as he had done spontaneously before. He wanted desperately to comfort her and yet, he knew he couldn't. Shouldn't. He was not free to have the life others took so for granted. He had made that choice many years ago. And now it was too late. He watched until she slipped back beneath the light blanket and was out of his sight.

He tossed irritably in the sleeping bag.

Unable to dismiss her from his mind, it was many hours before the gray fingers of sleep pulled the misty cobwebs over his eyelids and drew him into a restless, tormented slumber.

4

. . .come forth into the light of things.
                                    Wordsworth

S unlight streamed through the long, narrow castle windows. It threw a bright beam across Camilla's face and cast a myriad of sparkling light dancing in her golden hair. She stirred, stretched, and then as though it suddenly dawned on her that she was in Claire Castle with Dak, sat up so that she could see the sleeping bag across the room.

But it was gone. Folded up and put neatly aside. She looked around the room. It was so quiet. She pushed the covers aside, got up, and went over to the window, gazing out as she had last night. Little puddles dotted the courtyard where potholes had long ago begun to erode away the earth, settling among the cracked bricks produced by harsh New England winters. A row of daffodils marched along one side of the walled courtyard.

Camilla wondered if the infamous Claire's gardener had planted them. Probably not, she decided giving an answer to the fleeting thought. He had certainly had other things on his mind. The hard rain had nearly flattened all the yellow blossoms, and she was delighted to see one flower waving jubilantly beneath the rays of the sunlight, dancing solo with a playful breeze.

A smile turned up the corners of her mouth. She turned suddenly, running across the floor toward the door. She'd get the flower for Dak. She had nothing else, no money, no name, but she would give him the spring flower as a small token of her appreciation.

She pulled open the door and stepped out onto the stone porch. The crackle of static sounded behind her. Then: "Galileo. Are you there?" Casper, the friendly ghost voice, permeated the room, dominating the silence.

Camilla waited.

"Galileo, please respond," came impatiently.

Should she answer? It was obvious to her that Dak had a secret, but should she interfere? Maybe he wouldn't appreciate it if she did, helpful though she intended it to be.

"Dammit, Galileo. Where are you?" came the persistent but disgruntled voice.

Camilla strode back across the room. At the desk, she hesitated, nibbling on the tip of her finger.

"Galileo --" It was even more disgruntled than ever.

She picked up the receiver. "Yes. I mean no. He isn't here right now."

"Who the hell are you?"

Before she could reply, Casper demanded, "Is this Goldilocks?"

"Yes."

"What the hell do you think you're doing? This is none of your business. Where is Galileo?"

"If you'd stop yelling at me, I'd tell you," she replied curtly. "I know this is none of my business," she echoed his words, "but you sounded urgent and I was trying to be helpful -- and polite," she added, "which is more than you are doing."

There was silence at the other end.

She continued, her voice softer this time. "Dak . . . Galileo is not here at the moment. I don't know where he went, but I'm sure he'll be back shortly. Would you like me to have him contact you?"

Casper cleared his throat, regaining his composure.

"Yes, if you would, please."

"Certainly. Goodbye," Camilla said.

For just a second, the line was silent except the ever-present crackling. "Goldilocks?"

"Yes, Sir?" Camilla didn't know why she responded in that manner. She had the impression Casper was older, dignified, demanding respect from those around him.

His voice softened. "I'm sorry if I was sharp," he said simply.

Camilla smiled. "Apology accepted," she murmured.

Fancying she could see a smile stretch across a broad face, she repeated, "Bye."

"Bye, Goldilocks." And the communication was broken.

Camilla laid down the receiver and retraced her steps to the stone porch of the courtyard. She stood for a moment breathing in the air that always smelled so good after hard rain.

Stretching languidly, she scampered across the bricked courtyard to the row of battered daffodils. Camilla bent, snapped the one vibrant bloom loose, holding it to her nose. Daffodils really had no scent, and she knew that. It was just an automatic reaction to smell a flower. The sun was warm, the rays seeping through the light material of the poet shirt to caress her skin with welcome familiarity.

Shielding her eyes from the sun, Camilla surveyed the castle. It was a fanciful miniature replication of a medieval castle. Its two-storied, square, centered section was topped on the roof edge with square-notched battlements, mimicking the architectural decoration so necessary for firing upon aggressors in medieval times. The center section was flanked by a wing on one side, gutted by the fire of a vagrant, and a tower on the other that rose a story above the rest of the edifice. The rooftop of the tower was crenellated as well. Camilla smiled, loving the old world look of the castle. It was so solid in this day of too many cookie-cutter houses.

She breathed a sigh, raising her face to the warmth of the sun. She felt good this morning, her spirits rising like the sun in the clear blue sky. Impulsively, she twirled like a dancer, holding the daffodil between slender fingertips. The poet shirt floated with her supple movements and when she stretched both arms up, up over her head, the white fabric rose as well. Her shapely legs were exposed to the hip where the rest of her torso disappeared provocatively beneath the hem of the white shirt.

A small bird fluttered overhead, dispersing the false sense of lightheartedness that the clear day had teased her into feeling. Camilla dropped her arms and hurried toward the castle door.

She'd barely had time to make the bed when Dak returned. So soon, in fact, that Camilla wondered if he had been nearby and had seen her impromptu little dance in the courtyard. But his features were unreadable as he said, "Good morning. How do you feel today?"

"Better, thank you."

His eyebrows raised. "Anything?"

She knew he referred to her memory, and she shook her head solemnly.

He changed the subject. "I'm sure you'd like a bath. Ours is a bit archaic, but we've plenty of hot water. I'll show you where it is."

Camilla started to follow him, then remembered her flower. She retrieved it from the stand, holding it out to Dak. "Here. This is for you. I found it out by the courtyard wall. I wanted you to have it. Daffodils are a touch of sunshine, don't you think?"

He reached to take it but curled his strong hand around hers, dark blue eyes holding firmly to green ones. "Thanks," he responded softly. "I saw it dancing in the sunlight. Sweet of you. It's something I shall never forget."

Camilla's eyes clung to his. Though his words implied reference to the daffodil, she had the deep impression that it was her dancing in the sunlight that he meant. His dark blue gaze held hers for a long, almost breathless moment. Was he waiting for her to acknowledge it? She chose to change the subject. "Casper called."

He loosened his hold, accepting the flower. "Who?" Dark eyebrows darted upward.

"Your friend." She pointed to the radio. "He has no name. Just a ghost voice, so I call him

Casper." She waited for Dak to explain who Casper was and his real name. But he did neither.

"What did he say?" he asked.

"He wants you to call him back. In fact, he was a little upset that I answered, but I explained I was only trying to be helpful."

"Thank you. I'll reach him later. But first, let me show you to the castle bath."

And that dismissed adroitly any chance of learning who Casper was and how he fit into the mystery that cloaked Dak as comprehensively as the black cape he wore thrown around his shoulders. She followed his footsteps beyond the bed/living area through a gigantic kitchen that, if equipped with modern appliances, would have been any woman's dream.

Down the hall, Dak thrust open a door that still held the original carved wood handle with brass trimming. He stepped back, allowing her to pass. She peered in. Another large room. All the comforts of home, except the facilities were quaint. Camilla looked for a tub or shower, saw none.

"Where's the tub?" she asked, looking up at Dak.

He pointed.

She followed the pointing finger.

Dak took her arm, drawing her into the room and across the white and black marbled floor. In a corner was a large square well. It was tiled in aqua blue with a white border that had lost its pristine brightness over the years. Three steps led down to the well. Above it, on the wall were the faucets, long gooseneck affairs. A smile spread across Camilla's face, and she clapped her hands in delight. "A sunken tub! How enchanting!"

Dak grinned at her pleasure. "Sorry, there's

no shower. I'm assuming you can make do with this?"

"It's marvelous," she enthused. "Someone should restore this place. There are too many wonderful features going to waste. I hate to see lovely old houses like this decaying away into ashes."

Dak nodded. "I know. It has a personality all its own, doesn't it?"

"Wonder why no one has bought it to restore?"

"Its size and the fact that it's a bit on the outskirts of town." He looked around as though seeing it for the first time. "Though, you know, it does have certain elements that would make it a perfect inn with enough rooms to give every suite a private bath."

"No," Camilla said firmly. "That's too cold. It should remain a residence, with a nursery, and rooms for children. It has charm and . . . and, as you said, personality."

He reached into a built-in, recessed wall unit, withdrawing towels and washcloth. He handed them to her. Thoughtfully, his eyes flowed over her. "I remember a box of clothing stored in the atttic. I've no idea their vintage, but I'll go get them. Maybe there's something in there you can make use of until you're laundry arrives."

"Thank you."

Dak strode to the door. "Take your time. Relax as long as you want in our Roman tub. There is a pile of boxes and crates in the attic, so it'll take me a while to rummage around." He gave her an exaggerated wave to enjoy and left the room.

Camilla watched him go, closing the door behind him.

She went over, pushed in the plug that dangled from a chain, and turned on the faucets. Yipes! The water was hot. She turned on more cold. Adjusting it to her liking, the tub began to fill. Slipping out of the poet shirt, she ran more water in the sink on its pedestal frame where painted green ivy trailed down its sides. She stuffed the poet shirt in to soak. She'd see what was available in the box, and later today she'd have her own clothing. The least she could do was return his shirt laundered.

She went down the steps where the water was rapidly filling the well and dipped her toes in. Perfect. So thinking, she sank into the soothing warmth. How good to just lie there and soak. She unwrapped the gauze from around her forehead, laying it aside on the floor above her for disposal, and leaving the square patch over her temple. That still hurt to the touch, and she cringed to disturb it.

Some minutes later, while she lay soaking, she heard a light tapping at the door. "I'll just leave this box here by the door," Dak called in to her. "Can you manage?"

"Yes. Thank you."

She heard his footsteps receding and settled back into the depths of the sunken well. Bathing in leisurely fashion, she thought of the enigmatic Dak. An air of mystery enveloped him like the cloak he wore last evening. He was very careful not to allow her to know too much. She wondered again about his connection with Casper. That they were in the planning stage of something secretive was obvious. She wondered what it could be. He didn't seem like a law breaker. She felt in her heart that he could not do anything wrong. But one never knows. Probably Jack the Ripper's mother felt the same way about him.

Unbidden, his voice, soothing and gentle, came to mind calling her "baby" as he'd done last night during her weeping spell. He'd been so sweet, so tender. Camilla couldn't deny that she was drawn to him, that there was an unmistakable attraction between them.

She allowed herself to think of him romantically. She thought of his lips, firm, finely drawn like the aristocratically chiseled jaw. His hands were gentle. Very much aware of that fact, she sensed he could be passionate as well.

Her hormones had begun a persistent humming, and she allowed her fantasy full range, imagining him coming into the room and joining her in this enormous tub big enough for two. Her fanciful daydreams, fanned by a prolific imagination, intertwined with the throbbing in her veins which she was keenly aware was threatening to grow into a full blown storm. She must stop this nonsense. For God's sake. She didn't even know the man, and here she was sharing her bath with him!

God only knew what he was hiding from in this crumbling castle. He could be a murderer! But a little voice chastised her for that thought. No. Dak was no murderer. But he was dangerous just the same with those unsettling blue eyes and gentle hands that caressed her body, tantalizing her in the most seductive way. Yet, he did it so impersonally, as though she were an inanimate object.

She sat up with a splash, reaching for the shampoo, determined to scrub those erotic thoughts out of her head.

She worked the lather into her hair vigorously, trying hard to put him out of her mind.

She was rinsing her hair when, like a flashbulb recording a scene, a picture flashed into her mind. She saw herself running up a country lane. It was storming. Lightning flashed and rain poured. A pocketbook hung over her right shoulder. She saw herself look up and her mouth open as if to scream. And then, the memory went blank. But Camilla had gained one tiny bit of information. She had a purse on her shoulder before the tree limb struck. That meant it was probably under the limb, knocked from her shoulder or dislodged as she fell.

Excited about the fragmentary bit of recall, she leaned forward, jerking the chain with the stopper, climbed out of the tub, grabbed a towel and sailed out of the room.

"Dak! Dak!" she called, running toward the living area while trying to twist the towel into a secure knot at her bosom.

Alarmed, Dak came running from the upper regions of the house. He met her in the hall. "What's the matter?" His eyes flicked over her attire and then back to her excited features. "What is it?"

"I've remembered something. When I was running in the storm, I had a pocketbook over my shoulder. That means it must have fallen off when I was struck and is lying under the tree branches." She paused for breath, reaching out to him, laying her hands palm down on his chest. "Dak," she whispered, "if we can find my shoulder bag, then I can discover my name. Remember I told you I had put a pair of jeans in a suitcase? I must have had a car to be carrying a suitcase."

"Right," he said, quick to understand the inference. He gripped her arms, "You have a car, you have to have a driver's license. Bingo! We're about to discover who you are, Goldilocks."

Their contact, his hands on her arms, her hands on his chest, suddenly took on epic proportions, rendering them both speechless. The touch that had been spontaneous and innocent suddenly became the center of their emotions, and they both fell silent. Dak stood looking down into her eyes, she looking up into his. The moment was charged with electricity.

It took a great deal of restraint for him to say quietly, "Get dressed. We'll go look."

He released her, deeply conscious of her hands slipping down and away from his chest.

"I . . . I," she fumbled for words, finally blurting, "I'll be right back." She whirled and fled down the hall.

He stood there watching her with his hands knotted into fists, until she disappeared through the bathroom door. He ran his hand through his hair, blowing air from pursed lips, chastising himself, knowing that he had been very close to flicking that towel from around her.

Camilla rummaged in the box, knowing it would be too much to expect to find lingerie. However, there seemed to be a mixture of eras represented, and she suspected some youngster had used the contents for dressup. Among the items was a long Victorian dress with rows of ivory lace trimming the full, mutton sleeves and dancing across the bodice. Camilla smiled, lifting it from the box and holding it before her. The full-length mirror in the walnut armoire threw back her image. A smile crossed her features again.

Quickly, she bent to search for a belt of some sort and discovered a pink sash lying amid a bunch of lace edged hankies wrapped in tissue. The dress was lined in a fabric long since yellowed with age, but she didn't care. She was confident the material would hide her nakedness beneath it. There were more distressing things than being without lingerie. Even the revelation her memory had sparked was overshadowed by the encounter in the hall. That had left her much more rattled.

She undid the fold at her breast and let the towel fall, very much aware that this very act had been reflected in those deep blue eyes. Heart tripping a staccato beat, Camilla swallowed for she knew as sure as she was standing here that had he done so, she would have made no move to stop him.

A frown drew the corner of her mouth up, wondering if she were going to like herself when she learned her identity. Had she been easy? The thought scared the hell out of her. She didn't want to be that kind of person, but she didn't seem to have much restraint where Dak was concerned.

Quickly, she slipped the Victorian dress over her head, settling it around her naked hips. Lacking a brush or comb, she ran her fingers through her hair and slipped her feet back into the heels she had been wearing. She noted that they had been cleaned of mud and dirt and wondered when Dak had done that. Not wanting to ask him for detergent, she grabbed up the bar of soap. It would have to do and rinsed out the poet shirt before she left the bathroom.

She walked slowly down the hall, entering the room soundlessly. Dak was at the radio. Recognizing Casper's voice on the line, she waited just inside the doorway.

"Dak, this is serious business."

Camilla was strongly conscious of the imploring note in Casper's voice.

"I'm well aware of that, but I can't ignore this situation either," Dak replied, irritation making his words sharp.

"Can't you send her to a hotel? Send the bill here."

"Money is not the issue." The words were grated.

"She simply can't stay there."

"What do you expect me to do?" Dak's voice was agitated. "The poor girl is injured. She doesn't know who she is or who her people are. I can hardly throw her out into the street."

Casper let that pass, saying quietly, "You are putting her in grave danger."

Dak ran his hand over his face and then through his hair in a purely frustrated motion. "I can't let her face this alone," he murmured. "Just give me a couple of days. I should be able to locate her family by then."

Casper swore, snapping irritably, "How the hell can I grant you time when I have no idea myself when this thing will happen. They could strike at any time."

"I know. I know," Dak was trying to soothe him now. "Look, I promise you, she won't be involved. Will you just trust me on this?"

There was no answer.

Dak asked softly, "Have I ever let you down?"

The voice acquieced with a sigh that rattled across the static. "All right, Dak, but for God's sake, be careful. Maybe I should come out now."

"No," he replied quickly. "Let's just stick to our plan. I'll alert you if it's necessary."

Seconds later, the static quit, and Dak replaced the receiver. He stood there silently for a moment, then turned, and saw Camilla.

His eyes flowed over her, lingering on the Victorian dress. Quietly, he asked, "You heard?"

She nodded.

"I'm sorry."

She came forward, forgetting their earlier meeting, seeking only to absolve him of any blame. "It's not your fault. It is obvious that you and your friend, Casper, are engaged in some mission. I am the one who has imposed on your kindness, so you owe me no apology. Actually," she said with a slight lifting of her shoulders, "it is I who owe you the apology. Please don't defend me anymore. When I find my shoulder bag, then I will return home and be out of your life, and you can get on with whatever it is you're trying to do."

"Goldilocks -- " he began.

She reached up, placing her fingertips over his lips. "It's all right," she said softly. "Now come on, show me where I got clobbered."

He caught up her hand in a nonchalant manner, and they went outside.

"Do you ride?" Dak asked, drawing her toward a stone building beyond the left wing of the castle.

Her brow knitted. "I'm not sure, but I think so. Is that a stable?"

"Sure is. I keep my horse there."

She swung her head to look at him. "You have a horse?"

"I forgot," Dak said. "You have no memory of my riding up the lane last night just before you were hit."

"You rode up on horseback?" she murmured. "How quaint. I don't remember the horse, but I do recall thinking, when I woke up and saw you, that you were a Knight from King Arthur's Court," she confessed.

Dak chuckled. "You did look rather startled. I had been to a practice session for the jousting tournament over at the carnival grounds. Say," he flung a look down at her, "maybe you'd like to go to the fair. The joust isn't until the weekend, but you might enjoy the fair and the preliminaries. Want to go? It could be fun."

"Sure. I'd love to go."

There seemed to be no question to either of them that she would still be there by week's end.

They reached the stable, and Dak opened the heavy wooden double doors with massive wrought iron hinges and hasp. As soon as the doors were flung wide, they were greeted by pawing and snorting from the raven black stallion with bright, glittering eyes.

"Oh, he's beautiful," Camilla breathed, stroking the animal's nose. He nuzzled her shoulder playfully.

"I call him Rajah," Dak told her.

"Rajah," she murmured. "I like it. It suits him."

"We could take him down to the end of the lane if you like?" Dak offered. "Take just a minute to saddle him."

"Yes," she nodded, "let's."

"You're welcome to take him out while you're here if you'd like," he offered while saddling the stallion.

"Thanks. Maybe I will sometime."

A short time later, they cantered across the bricked courtyard, Rajah's delicate prancing echoing round the walled interior. Clip-clop, clip-clop. Her skirt spread out in a frothy sweep just as it had no doubt done in the past. Camilla turned from her perch in front of Dak to smile up at him.

With the castle in the background, they looked like they were from another century.

Camilla's hair was as golden as the sunlight that splashed down all around, lapping at the puddles created from last evening's hard rains. It filtered through the branches of the trees, creating a dappled pattern on the dirt road.

It took only minutes to traverse the short distance to the bend in the lane where the limb had splintered from the tree and fallen to earth, striking Camilla as it fell. Dak eased her to the ground, then swung down to join her.

A quick glance was all that was necessary to tell them the shoulder bag was not anywhere on the dirt road.

"Perhaps it's under the tree limb?" Camilla suggested hopefully.

"I pulled that limb off of you and tossed it onto the roadside. I doubt if it's under it," he told her gently.

"Well, maybe it got caught on a branch or something."

"Maybe," he said, though in his heart he didn't think it likely. "We'll look just in case."

They searched in and around among the leaves and branches. Dak even moved the heavy limb again. No pocketbook.

Camilla's mouth was drawn down in disappointment. "I was so sure we'd find it," she murmured.

"I know," he said, resting his hand comfortingly on her shoulder. "Probably some animal has carried it off. It could be anywhere."

"If only I could remember," she said in

frustration, putting the heels of her hands to her temples, and in the process hit the wound on her head. She winced.

The futile gesture brought the covered wound to Dak's attention. "It's been bleeding again. Let's go back to the castle, and I'll put a clean bandage on it."

She nodded solemnly.

Dak climbed astride Rajah, who whinnied softly as though sympathetic to the desolate atmosphere and stood patiently as Dak reached down to lift Camilla up in front of him.

They returned to the castle, Rajah's footbeats striking against the earthen lane in an even more melancholy resonance.

5

As doubtful thoughts,
and rash-embraced despair,
And shuddering fear,
and green-eyed jealousy.

Shakespeare

While Dak cleansed the wound again, he said, "It looks better today. You'll be fit as a fiddle in no time."

"If I could just get my memory back."

"You will, Goldilocks," he said firmly.

"But what if I don't?" She raised scared green eyes to him. "What does a person who has amnesia do? Just take another name and begin life again at that point, with no knowledge of their life before? Not even knowing if you've left behind someone who loves you . . . someone whom you love." Her eyes held his. "Surely there is someone who loves me, perhaps someone I love," she

48

whispered, ending on a wistful, melancholy note. "Everyone has someone."

"Come on, stop this," Dak admonished. "Of course, there is someone, lots of people, who love you. And they're all probably frantic at this time. You have to start thinking positively." He finished putting a clean bandage on her temple, and striving to change the subject, inquired, "Did you find yourself anything for breakfast?"

She shook her head.

"Well, too late now," he dismissed it jovially. "We might as well go for brunch." He drew her up from the chair. "Can you cook?"

"I have no idea."

"Well, we're about to find out." He grinned at her, and she couldn't resist returning it. "It's the same as riding a bike," he continued. "Once you know how, you never forget."

They stood in the large kitchen. Dak threw out his hand. "Root through the fridge and the cupboards. We'll get something to eat, and then I'll go back out and find your pocketbook. It has to be there someplace."

He put his finger beneath her chin, lifting her face up to him. "I'll promise to find it, Goldilocks, if you'll promise to stop worrying. Everything will work out, you'll see. Promise?" he urged softly.

She smiled. "Promise," she whispered.

"Good. Now let's find something to eat. I'm starved."

"By jove, you can cook!" Dak declared cheerily as they finished their meal.

"Oh, right. A real challenge," Camilla tossed back, rising to clear away the remains of the plate of sliced ham, cheese and tomatoes, and thick slices of   dark pumpernickel bread.

But Dak reached out, touching her hand, detaining her.

"Sit down," he said, "we need to talk."

He sounded so deadly serious that Camilla sank back into the chair without a word. Her eyes searched his face.

He sat there a moment just looking at her, but Camilla noticed his eyes flickering like something weighed heavily on his mind. Silently, she sat there, waiting for him to speak.

His lips twisted from side to side, as though mulling his thoughts, then he forced a smile at her.

"You're starting to scare me," she said, alarm registering in the green eyes. "Dak? What is it?" She leaned toward him. "You're not in trouble with the law, are you?" Her words were spoken sotto voce.

"On occasion," he replied lightly, then seeing her surprised expression and hearing the tiny gasp, he leaned across the table to touch her hand. "No, not in the way you're thinking."

Still, he noted, she didn't relax.

"Goldilocks, as you have gathered from the radio messages, I'm not here on vacation, though we've made it appear that way, and it is one of the reasons I'm participating in the jousting tournament. But actually," he lowered his voice, "I'm here on a mission. And now it seems, I have to trust you as much as you had to trust me. And since we know absolutely nothing about each other, I, like you did, must rely on my instincts."

Though she didn't speak, she clung to his every word, knowing he was about to reveal the pieces to his enigmatic persona.

"It seems that since Fate has dropped you on my doorstep -- "

"Your lane," she interjected softly, though the point held no real value.

He nodded. "All right, lane. My point is, Goldilocks, that I think we're stuck with each other for a few days. As soon as we locate your purse, I'll have Moth run your driver's license card number through our computers. See if we can find out anything about you."

"Moth?"

"My partner. Casper."

"Oh."

"He will contact us as soon as he learns anything."

She nodded solemnly, knowing this was just the beginning, sensing he had something much more unsettling to impart.

"I'm going to take you into my confidence, but first, you must give me your solemn vow not to discuss with anyone what I will tell you."

A giant lump leaped to her throat, wondering at the magnitude of what he was about to share with her.

Dak's eyes flowed slowly over her, and he finally said, "I am an undercover agent. Someone is dealing in illegal arms that are being smuggled to terrorist countries. We have traced it here and expect a large shipment to be picked up by boat somewhere along the coast. We've been on their trail for months. I can't allow anything to jeopardize this operation. Do you understand?"

Camilla nodded. "You can trust me, Dak," she said. "You must believe that."

His eyes held hers, and his dark head moved up and down. "You must also understand,

51

Goldilocks, that you have to stay out of the way. The agency would take strong actions if a civilian were injured during one of our operations."

"I won't get in your way," she promised.

"I've been watching the bay for weeks. So far, there've been no boats bringing in smaller deliveries. We're sure we have the right spot earmarked. There are many caves along this stretch of coast where they could hide contraband. I just have to keep watching until I can learn their hideout. I'm renting the castle, pretending interest in purchasing the property so as not to create any curiosity in the village. No one must know who I really am."

"How did you get the name Galileo?"

"I have an antique, collapsible telescope that belonged to my grandfather. When I initially joined the agency, I used it instead of binoculars. My colleagues first attached the name to me. Over the years, it stuck."

"And Moth? Your partner."

"He's been with the force twenty-five years. The men used to josh him about being drawn to danger like a moth to a flame. Hence, the name. He took me under his wing and taught me everything. We have both undergone highly specialized training." He grinned, thinking back on it. "We have gained access into more high-security buildings than you can shake a stick at. Moth is clever, courageous, and self-reliant."

Camilla felt those same qualities fit Dak as well.

"Moth is not just my partner," Dak said quietly. "He's also my best friend."

"How long have you been on the force?"

"Twelve years."

"What is Moth's real name?" she asked inquisitively.

Dak was silent, and she held up a hand. "Sorry. Guess you can't tell me that. I was just curious," she finished, as though in explanation of her off-handed question. "I always think of him as Casper anyway," she said in a light-hearted manner.

A little smile flitted across Dak's mouth. Despite the moment's hesitation, he told her anyway. "It's Earl Babcock."

They lapsed into a moment's silence, then she said seriously. "Dak, please don't ever think that I would betray your trust. Even after I'm gone . . . when you find my purse, my license will have my address . . . I'll go back home to that other life and though I won't forget you, I will never mention you or your mission to anyone. I want you to know that."

Dak's dark head moved up and down. "I already know that, Goldilocks, otherwise I would never have told you." He pushed back from the table, rising to his feet. "Now let me go find that infamous shoulder bag."

"I'll clean up," Camilla offered, also rising.

A muted knock from the front room resounded, and blue eyes met green. In a split second, Dak had come around the table to where Camilla stood. "At the first sign of trouble, get out the back door and into the woods," he whispered hurriedly, as he grabbed up her plate, glass and utensils, and thrust them into a cupboard.

She nodded, though her heart was thumping in her chest as she followed his swift actions in concealing the extra place setting.

The knock sounded again.

"Stay here, and don't make a sound."

A voice called out, "Dak? Are you home? It's Marielena."

At the newcomer's first word, the rigidity left Dak's body. He bent to Camilla. "It's okay. It's Marielena."

"Who's Marielena?" Camilla squeaked, still rattled from the possibility that the knock at the door might have been of a hostile nature.

"She's a gypsy girl from the carnival. She's probably brought your laundry."

A blank look rested on Camilla's features.

"I sent your clothing out, remember?" he whispered hurriedly. "I don't get to town much. Marielena and her mother take care of my laundry." He flung the last back over his shoulder as he went to admit the girl at the door.

Camilla watched from the doorway as Marielena swept in, her arms full of freshly laundered and pressed clothes. Dak took them from her, setting them on a chair.

The gypsy girl moved with a fluid motion across the floor. Instead of sitting in a chair, she perched herself on the desk, pulling her long floral skirt up above her knees as she crossed her legs. Legs that were long and bronzed, and she was very much aware of Dak's eyes on them. She put her hands behind her, palms down on the desk, and leaned backward, pointed breasts thrust outward, straining against the thin fabric of her off-the-shoulder bright yellow peasant blouse. Her black eyes skimmed over Dak's face to his lips, allowing her eyes to rest reflectively there, at which point she ran a pink tongue over her own vividly painted mouth. Her black gaze moved onward, languidly, gliding over broad shoulders, lingering on firm, narrow hips. In those sultry, dark depths was naked desire.

"I looked for you all day," she said.

"I was busy," Dak replied.

"They had a practice run for the joust."

"There'll be another one tomorrow."

Her gaze held his slowly, then she slid off the desk, allowing the puff of one sleeve of the blouse to slip further down her shoulder, exposing the soft flesh of her breast. She moved across the short expanse with a slow, undulating movement and leaned against Dak.

"Meet me tonight," she whispered.

"No. I can't."

"Then I will come here," she offered.

"No. No," Dak said hurriedly. "Perhaps another time."

She ran her fingertips up the back of his neck. "But Dak --" she began.

Camilla marched into the room, nonchalantly announcing, "I finished cleaning up the kitchen, Dak."

The gypsy girl turned toward Camilla, keeping her body firmly pressed where she leaned into Dak. Her dark eyes narrowed as they flowed over Camilla, petite and rose-like, in her Victorian gown. "Playing house with little girls, are we?" she murmured.

Dak flung a frown at Camilla, grabbed Marielena by the arm, pulling her through the doorway and outside beyond Camilla's vision and range of hearing.

It was several minutes before he returned. And when he did, he stood surveying her with one hand on his hip and fire in his eyes. "What . . . may I ask, was that all about?"

Camilla turned her back on him. "I owed

you one. Now we're even."

"What the hell are you talking about?" he demanded.

"You saved my life, now I saved yours."

He looked at her aghast.

And she conceded, "Well, maybe I didn't save your life. But I did save you from yourself," she proclaimed, shaking a finger at him.

"How's that?" he flung back.

"You were making no attempt to get out of the clutches of that man-eating shark!"

He scowled. "Didn't you even think," he asked pointedly, "that maybe -- just maybe -- I might not want to be saved from her?"

That caused Camilla to frown. "Oh," she murmured, surveying him in a quizzical fashion as though that idea had never occurred to her. She considered it for a second, took a deep breath, and retraced her steps to the kitchen.

"Where are you going?" Dak called after her.

"To clean up the kitchen."

"I thought you already did that."

"No. I haven't."

"But you said you had --" He followed her into the next room.

"That was just an excuse. To help you out of a situation I thought you wanted out of."

"I can take care of myself."

She turned to face him, her mouth open to respond. But she clamped it shut and began to gather up the dishes.

Dak stood watching her, wondering what had been on the tip of her tongue. He liked sparring with her, liked the fire that leaped to her eyes that made her eyes appear even greener. In fact, they were a very bright, distinct shade of green. He smiled inwardly. By God! Goldilocks was jealous!

He almost made the observation aloud, but just before giving voice to the thought, he said softly, "I'll go search for your pocketbook now."

"Want me to come with you?" she asked half-heartedly.

He shook his head. "Don't forget the dishes we stashed in the cupboard," he said, and left the room.

Camilla rooted among the cupboards until she found the detergent. In a short time, she had everything cleaned and put away and went back to the living area.

The clothes Marielena had brought were still on the chair where Dak had put them. She claimed her own clothing from the stack and carried them to the stand beside the bed. Her face turned pink, mentally conjuring up a picture of Dak removing her underwear. She pulled herself out of the fantasy quickly, before it could blossom into an almost tangible image, and grow out of her control. She put the lingerie in the drawer of the stand, seeing no reason to change her attire. After all, it was impossible for Dak to know that beneath her long dress, she was nude. She couldn't help but admit to herself that she enjoyed the relative freedom, if one could call it freedom when one was wrapped in yards of linen and lace.

An hour passed before she heard Dak's footsteps on the stone porch. Her heart began a rapid staccato. Had he found her shoulder bag? Would she now discover her identity and leave the castle and Dak? Her heart did a curious little somersault which left her breathless.

The doorknob turned and Dak came in. He held up his right hand. Clutched in his grip was her shoulder bag.

"You found it," she said, suddenly very nervous.

Dak grinned. "I sure did. Some animal had dragged it off." He came across the room to where she'd sunk down onto the bed. "It's a little soggy from the rain, and slightly gnawed, but it didn't come open. Everything should be there." He handed it out to her.

Camilla's eyes met his as she reached to accept it. A lump had formed in her throat that, along with her furiously beating heart, made her feel suffocated. Her fingers worked at the clasp and then the zippered pocket. Inside, she saw a gold compact nestled next to a black eel-skin wallet. A shaking hand reached in to withdraw the compact. The initials C. L. were engraved in flowing script on the front.

"C. L.," she murmured, tracing the letters with her fingertip.

After a moment, she laid the compact aside and drew out the wallet. She opened it slowly, feeling strangely about being on the brink of discovering her own name. She finally found the card.

Dak watched her staring at her driver's license. He saw her close her eyes momentarily, as though gathering her composure, then she raised luminous green eyes to him.

6

. . . will you not stay . . .

Hodgson

"**M**y name is Camilla Lloyd."

"Well," Dak breathed, sinking down next to her on the bed. "Camilla, huh? Pretty name. It suits you."

She smiled wanly.

"Course, Goldilocks suits you, too," he said lightly, for she looked so deadly serious.

The pocketbook slid from her lap and she turned, burying her face against Dak's chest. It seemed a natural thing to do to put his arms about her. He could feel her trembling. "Hey, come on," he said, looking down on her. "This is supposed to be a triumphant moment."

"I'm so scared, Dak," she whispered. "I really thought once I knew my name, everything would come rushing back. But it hasn't."

"Maybe you're trying too hard," he

suggested.

She moved out of his arms, reaching down to pick up her shoulder bag that lay in a mottled brown heap at her feet. She cradled it in her lap and flipped open her wallet again. In the clear plastic slot next to her driver's license was a registration card. She withdrew it and held it out to Dak. "I have a car," she said quietly.

"So I see," he replied, scanning the small square card. "And not just any car. A Corvette." He grinned, trying to entice a smile from her. "You have good taste."

Only one corner of her mouth drew up as though she had no time to concentrate on such banal chatter. "My license gives my address as Nashua," she said softly. "So you know what that means."

"No. I don't see that it has any significant meaning."

"But it does," she said emphatically. "If my address, my home, is Nashua, then that means I was running away from something."

"Now, Goldi - Camilla. It doesn't mean any such thing," Dak stated.

"I had a suitcase, Dak. Why would I have a suitcase, not a hundred miles from home, if I weren't running from something?"

"Perhaps you were going to visit someone," he answered quietly.

She shook her head adamantly. "I don't think so. Something is telling me I was running away from something."

"Maybe you were on your way home from a short vacation," he suggested.

Still, she shook her head. "I was running away," she murmured solemnly.

"You didn't kill anyone, did you?" Dak

asked with a grin, trying to dispel the solemn moment.

"I don't think so," she replied seriously.

"I was joking," Dak said, giving her a little shake. "Of course, you haven't killed anyone," he finished firmly.

"How do you know?"

"Instinct," he answered shortly. "I've learned to trust it."

"Are you usually right . . . your instincts, that is?"

"Almost a hundred percent."

She frowned, making rows of tiny creases in her forehead.

"What's wrong? You don't believe my instincts?" he asked.

She tried to smile at him, but it was a bare whisper. "It's not that," she said. "It's blue eyes."

Dak shook his head. "Blue eyes? What about blue eyes?"

"I'm not sure, but even though yours are different in some way, every time I look into them, this awful feeling of sadness engulfs me. I can remember when I first woke up and saw you looking down on me, and I saw your blue eyes, I wanted to cry."

Dak made no reply.

"Not much to go on, is it," she asked wistfully. "My name is Camilla Lloyd, and blue eyes make me sad. Not much of a past, is it?" She suddenly caught her breath, her green eyes growing wide and somewhat wild.

"What? You've recalled something?" Dak asked, ducking his head down to peer up into her face.

"Dak." Her lower lip was trembling, and

Dak knew she was about to cry. "You don't suppose I'm crazy? Maybe I escaped from a mental institution."

He shook his head. "You're not crazy, Goldilocks. You got a nasty crack on the skull, and you've got temporary loss of memory."

"But --"

Still, he shook his head. "Sorry, you're completely sane. And you're going to have to deal with whatever is haunting you from your past . . . blue eyes and all."

"But --" she repeated.

"No but's," he said firmly. "Besides, escaped mental patients don't drive around in new Corvettes."

"Maybe I stole it," she offered.

He shook his head slowly. "Nope. Besides, you have a registration to prove it's yours. You'd have been caught if it were stolen when you tried to register it."

She frowned, taking his words to heart, and replying as though she thought he expected an answer, or an admission. "I suppose you're right."

"Of course, I'm right. Face it, Sweetheart, you're sane." He flashed her a big grin, shooting his dark eyebrows up and down.

She laughed, shaking her head, then wrapped her arms around him and gave him a brief hug. "Thanks, Dak. You're great." She pushed away from him, conscious of his hands slipping away from her upper arms.

She rose, standing there looking down on him. "Well," she said with a sigh, "shouldn't I go home now or something? I have an address. It isn't as though I have no where to go."

He didn't answer, only shrugged his

shoulders as if it were her decision.

Camilla's eyes flowed over him. "I could call a cab. And later, when I remember where I left it, I can get my car."

She felt awkward. She didn't want to go, yet she knew she shouldn't stay. Dak had his job to consider. It was not fair of her to stay, no matter how comforting it was to have him near. The purse slipped from her grasp and hit the floor. It was a muted sound, yet it served to make them both very much aware that the time for their chance meeting was at an end, and the past few hours would soon only be a memory.

The next instant, Dak bent, swooping the purse up with one hand. "Don't go, Goldilocks," he uttered so softly Camilla cast a quick glance down at him, her heart skipping a beat, wondering if she'd heard him correctly.

He rose, handing her the pocketbook, his eyes holding hers. "Can't it wait a few days, at least until after the jousting tournament?"

"But . . . your mission. Casper . . . Moth. "

"If you go before you regain your memory, I'd only worry about you. Please," he whispered, his eyes clinging to hers, "wait awhile."

Camilla stifled the urge to fling herself into his arms. Instead, she said, "If you're sure. I would like to go to the Renaissance Faire and see the jousting tournament."

"Good." He drew a long sigh. "Now," he said, smiling down at her, "let's go for a walk. I'll show you around the castle grounds."

7

A pleasant walk, a pleasant talk,
Along the briny beach.

Carroll

With a nonchalant motion, he caught her hand in his, taking it for granted that they were in agreement, and drew her towards the door.

He led her through the courtyard to the back of the castle. A flagstone path led through a wrought iron gate to a wooded area. It was a narrow forest that divided the house from the hillside overlooking the bay.

The much worn path meandering through the woods prompted her to ask, "Where does this path lead?"

"Not far. It comes out on a hillside overlooking the bay. It's a beautiful view."

"Is it where you go to watch the coastline

with your telescope?" she asked, dropping her voice despite the fact they were alone.

He nodded.

She could imagine him leaning against the girth of a tree, his cloak creating a sense of dark eminence, and his long fingers holding the slender telescope as he bent his dark head to peer through the lens. She peeped up at him as they emerged from the wooded area to the hillside. A light breeze teased the tiny wings of gray at his temples. Camilla's fingers longed to touch those distinguished wisps that feathered against his black hair. With an effort she turned her attention to the bay, lying still and somnolent in the wake of last night's storm.

She spied a small rowboat on the beach below them and called it to Dak's attention.

"I found it in one of the outbuildings. I've taken it out a couple of times." He shot a look down at her. "Want to go for a row?"

"Can we?"

"Sure. I'm King of the Castle, remember?" He grinned, catching up her hand, and pulling her along to the edge of the hill where there was a rusted, and somewhat rickety, wrought iron stairs that clung to the rocky hillside, snaking its way to the ground.

"The stairs are pretty steep, so be careful," he cautioned, stepping onto the iron stairs. Camilla followed and slowly, they made their way to the sandy beach below.

A patch of daisies grew in a small, sandy hillock along the bank of the hillside. It was a living tapestry of yellow, white, and green against the sand and gray stone of the rocky embankment, and Dak bent as they passed, snapped one from the wild profusion, and handed it to Camilla.

Accepting the flower, her eyes met his briefly, before he untied the rowboat from its mooring.

Camilla slipped off the cumbersome heels and stood barefoot in the sand, letting the shoes dangle by the back strap. Wadding the skirt of her equally cumbersome long dress into a ball, she clutched it under her arm, and mindful of her nakedness, was careful not to drag the skirt too high. Despite her precautions, it was difficult for Dak not to notice the long length of shapely leg peeping out of the folds of ivoried material.

Dak put his hand on her elbow to assist as she climbed over the side and sat down where he indicated. He gave the boat a heave, sending it out into the water, and scrambled aboard as it bobbled on the gently rolling surf.

Facing Camilla, Dak dipped the oars expertly, thrusting them with a languid motion over the clear surface. Windsongs and water music whispered across the blue water. In the distance, the tall masts above the sleek hull of a sailboat was visible, its sails billowing in the wind.

"This is so relaxing," Camilla said. "Isn't it beautiful out here?"

Dak nodded, his eyes flicking slowly over the landscape, coming to rest on a ship on the horizon.

Camilla had the impression that his work was constantly on his mind, and she said softly, "It is so peaceful out here, it's hard to believe that there is subterfuge taking place somewhere along this coast."

"Unfortunately," Dak answered her quiet observation, "it is going on more often than the average person realizes. Smuggling is not exclusive to weapons. It is a major problem with drugs. Even people." He saw Camilla's eyes grow wide and said, "The black market is as ugly as its name."

She studied his strong profile for a moment, liking the way the sunlight played over the chiseled jaw and danced with sensual highlights over arms that rippled with muscles as he manned the oars.

After a while, she asked in a low voice, "Who were you expecting when Marielena knocked at the door?"

His broad shoulders shrugged. "I don't know anyone here, except Marielena. It was merely a reflex action. A precaution. You learn to take them in my line of work. I'd forgotten about Marielena."

Camilla fell silent, wanting to ask where he had met the beautiful gypsy girl but feared he would quite likely tell her it was none of her business. Which it wasn't, so instead, she allowed her gaze to wander over the gray rock escarpment of the hillside.

"Look, Dak," she said, pointing to an old mansion hovering on the edge of the bluff.

Dak's head raised to the direction she pointed, and she knew he was observing with interest the old house perched high above them even though she could not see his eyes which were shielded from the sun with dark glasses. "Been a nice old place in its day," he murmured.

She nodded. "Still not as interesting as the castle."

He smiled. "No. I have to agree with you. The castle has a unique personality."

They rowed over the bay for a while longer

in leisurely silence. At length, Dak asked, "I have to compete in a jousting match tonight. Would you like to go with me? It won't take long, and we could do the carnival. What do you say?" He quirked an eyebrow at her.

She nodded her blond head. "Yes. I'd like to do that."

"Good. Okay if we grab a bite to eat there?"

Again, she nodded. "Sure. I haven't been to a carnival since I was a little girl. It will be fun."

Dak's head tilted quizzically. "You remember that from your past?"

She shook her head. "No, but it must be true because I spoke spontaneously."

Her brow furrowed, as he noted it often did, when she strived to remember bits of her fog-shrouded life.

"What?" he asked softly.

"If I went to a carnival when I was a little girl, my parents must have taken me."

He waited for her to continue, agreeing, "I'm sure they did."

"Then," she asked in an irate voice, "where are they?"

Dak opened his mouth to offer a reasonable answer, but she went on with an agitated toss of her blond head. "I mean, if they cared enough to take me to the carnival, that meant they were loving parents, right?" Again, she didn't wait for a reply. "Well, wouldn't you think they'd care enough to search for me?" she demanded.

"They probably are searching for you," Dak told her quietly.

"Do you think?" Again that little girl, wistful voice.

"No doubt," he answered firmly.

"Do you suppose," she asked softly, "if I saw my parents, it would make me remember who I am?"

"I don't know," he answered honestly.

"One thing I know for sure; I'm not married," she said softly.

He glanced up with a questioning look on his face.

Camilla held her hands out. "No rings," she said.

"So I noticed," he said softly.

"I wonder if I have a boyfriend," she murmured.

"No doubt, dozens," Dak told her.

But she frowned. "If there were someone special, surely I would remember him." She tilted her head. "Wouldn't I?"

Dak shrugged.

He heard a deep sigh flow across the short expanse from where she sat, and he gave a sharp thrust of the oars which sent them gliding across the bay. They reached the shore in a very short time.

Dak jumped out, pulling the boat onto the beach, and secured it to its mooring. Then he gave his hand to Camilla, as she climbed out onto the sandy shore.

Playfully, he winked down at her. "Race you to the ladder?"

She grinned. "You're on!" Releasing his hand, she was already running, clutching her skirt in one hand and her shoes in the other.

His long-legged stride overtook her midway, but she didn't care. Laughing, she reached the rusty stairway clinging precariously to the rocky hillside.

8

There arises the recognition of evil.

Lao-tzu

Standing in front of the old walnut armoire in the bathroom, Camilla studied her reflection in its full length mirror. She turned to the side. The dress fit her perfectly as though it had been made for her. Having rummaged through the box again, she'd found a slim, '50's sheath dress of pale blue.

Though Marielena had returned the freshly cleaned suit she had on when Dak found her, it seemed too severe for the carnival, and she had resorted to rooting through the attic box again. At least, this time she had lingerie, she thought with a grin. She let out a hoot of joy when she found, tucked at the very bottom of the box, a pair of sandals. She had to tighten the buckle as far as it would go, but all in all, the ensemble looked quite nice. Now that she had ironed out the years of wrinkles with an old relic of an iron that Dak had found in a kitchen cupboard, she felt quite pleased with the outfit.

With a pleased smile playing around her mouth, she stepped into the hallway. As she approached the main room of the castle, she could hear the soft crooning of a love song. It was the sound of another era, another generation, and she was suddenly curious about the music of Dak's choice.

The mellifluous notes of Nat King Cole's "Unforgettable" hovered in the air, seeming to dominate the cavernous space of the room, and she stopped just inside the doorway, listening. The voice emanated from an ancient relic of a record player. Dak stood quietly, pensively watching the record as it turned slowly on the worn turntable. He seemed lost in the melodious sound and the words that were crooned in a way that had mesmerized Nat's fans for decades.

Camilla watched him silently, allowing her gaze to gravitate slowly over his tall frame. He wore a black turtleneck knit shirt, and over it a jupon, a loose fitting, sleeveless tunic that gathered at the waist. Black trousers clung smoothly over firm hips, and black boots rose to his knees. As though to relieve the austerity of the somber outfit, he'd tied a lacy cravat around his neck. It cascaded in a frothy white mass down the center of his chest.

Detecting the muted rustle behind him, Dak turned slightly and saw Camilla.

His gaze flowed slowly over her, taking in the pale blue dress of an era that still looked fresh, and spring-like. The dress had a softly scooped neckline, and since she wore no necklace, it paid

71

accent to the smooth column of her neck. She looked like a flower that had just opened after a winter's slumber.

A slow, appreciative smile came over his mouth, as he surveyed her. Slowly, as though of its own volition, he raised his hand and held it out to her.

Acknowledging the invitation to dance, she said apologetically, "I don't know if I can dance."

"Well, let's see," he murmured, taking several steps toward her, his firm hand reaching for hers.

Camilla hesitated for only a fraction of a second.

Gently, Dak swept her into his arms, moving slowly around the room keeping time to the music. "What magic have you wrought from the attic box of discarded fashions? This morning Victorian, and now a perennial Jackie Kennedy favorite. Are you a chameleon, Goldilocks, as changeable as the wind?"

"If of a necessity," she answered softly, not sure he referred to her clothing.

Seconds later, he murmured close to her ear, "Nat's my favorite."

Camilla looked up at him. "Isn't he Natalie Cole's father?"

Dak's footsteps faltered for just a second. "Well, guess that proves without a doubt that we're from entirely different generations," he said with a frown.

"What do you mean?" she asked.

"Well, for one thing, I think of Natalie as the daughter of Nat King Cole. You think of him as Natalie's father." He was silent as they moved in perfect time. "He was one in a million with a voice as smooth as silk."

He glanced down at her. "You like Nat?"

"Nice," she answered shortly.

"Mr. Cole's music is perfect for dancing." Dak began to sing the words along with his idol. Camilla closed her eyes, leaning against Dak. His breath whispered over her senses, feathering across her temple and neck. She heard him stop singing, then felt his lips brush her temple in an almost absent minded way. She tipped her head to look up at him. The look in his eyes told her it had not been absent minded at all. He was in full control of his faculties and completely aware of his actions. The next moment, his lips had found their way to hers, and they rested there so softly, so sweetly that Camilla felt her heart tumble in a rather breathless way.

When he drew away, his eyes held hers, and he said, "If we're going to the fair, we'd better get going."

She nodded, reaching for the black helmet, banded in white that lay in readiness on the desk. A white feathered plume curved over the top of the helmet. Dak's distinguished dark looks lent an air of mystery to the image he was creating. She handed it to him. "Put it on," she said.

He complied, slipping the helmet over his dark head.

Camilla stared at the indigo blue eyes that held her gaze through the slit in the upper portion of the helmet. She could not help thinking that he looked like a character out of a child's picture book set in another place in time. She smiled to herself thinking what a romantic figure he cast, like a dark knight with a froth of lace at his throat, evoking quixotic chivalry.

Her smile deepened. "It suits you," she said

softly.

"Think so?" he asked casually, reaching for the black cloak she'd seen him wearing yesterday. With a nonchalant toss, he swung it round his shoulders. It settled around him, adding immensely to the sense of mystery and of an age long gone.

Before he offered her his arm, he removed the helmet, saying, "I'm riding Rajah over to the fairgrounds. Would you like to ride with me, or would you prefer to take my car?"

"Oh, I'd like to ride with you, if you don't mind."

"My pleasure, fair maiden," he replied in exaggerated tones, as he tucked her hand through his arm.

As they approached the stable, they could hear Rajah's low nicker. Saddled and ready to go, the horse was outfitted for the joust in a hooded, snow white blanket that contrasted with his sleek black coat. His flowing black tail was a raven flame that swished from side to side when they entered the archaic stone stable.

Dak led the stallion outside to the courtyard. Sitting astride the mighty animal, they were a picturesque pair. Dak's black outfit with the flowing black cape contrasted sharply with Rajah's white blanket. The breeze teased the froth of lace at Dak's throat as he bent to lift Camilla up in front of him.

Holding the helmet on her lap, they rode down the lane and turned onto a path that led through the woods and paralleled the road to the carnival grounds. Dusk was just beginning to gather when they arrived at the festival.

Small, colored bulbs lit the circle of the ferris wheel and other various rides that catered to the young set. Lights were strung from pole to pole, circling the area, lending additional illumination. A loud speaker sent squawking music, interrupted by varied announcements, to every corner of the fair grounds.

Children ran and played, their excited, high-pitched voices combined with parental cautions. The mingled smells of carnival foods filled their nostrils as Dak slid Camilla to the ground, then dismounted. He led Rajah to a stall next to other horses awaiting the call to the competition.

"Want to grab a burger or something first?" he asked, taking the helmet from her and setting it aside.

"Sure."

His hand caught up hers in a casual manner as they stepped into the mainstream of the affair. "Hamburger? Hot dog?" he asked.

"Either one. Whatever you prefer."

"Burger," he grinned. "With lots of pickles and onions, catsup, and mustard."

They passed a tent where a huge man, dressed as Henry the VIII, was hawking Renaissance-inspired, one-pound smoked turkey legs. The menu board offered peasant bread, apple dumplings, shish-kabobs with unidentifiable meats skewered together, as well as ales and mead to wash it all down.

Dak looked at Camilla in response to the man's offer. "The lady's choice," he told the hawkster.

"I don't think so!" Camilla laughed, spying someone trying to manage one of the huge turkey legs.

Laughing together, they moved on toward the hamburger tent where she stood at his side as he asked for double orders of burgers, fries, and cokes. While they waited, she called his attention to a group of people gathered round a table that held a whole roasted pig on an enormous platter in the center of the table.

"Our choice of food seems a bit boring," he chuckled, accepting their burger and fries from the vendor.

"That's all right," she grinned, "at least we know what we are eating."

Dak spied an empty table under the food tent and nodding in that direction, they wended their way through the milling crowd to it. The burgers were thick and juicy - if somewhat greasy - and spotting a tiny dribble of catsup on the corner of Dak's mouth, Camilla leaned over and dabbed at it with her napkin. He winked at her, sinking even white teeth into another juicy bite.

"Dak! I've been looking all over for you." Marielena swept down on them with a slender, ruddy-cheeked man in tow. "I saw Rajah in the stall, so I knew you had arrived." Her eyes flicked over Camilla but came to rest on Dak with that caressing look that smouldered from her dark, gypsy eyes. "This is Dimitri," she announced, indicating her companion.

Dak nodded curtly as Camilla murmured a polite, "How do you do?" conscious that Dak had visibly stiffened.

"I'm dancing tonight," Marielena purred. "Will you come see me?"

"Sure. Sure," Dak replied in an preoccupied manner.

Camilla noticed he'd pushed away his burger that he had been enjoying so much moments ago. It wasn't as if he had stopped eating for politeness' sake. It was as though he had lost his appetite. The thought crossed her mind, that if she weren't still at his house, perhaps he would have been here with the gypsy girl. With that notion lingering in her mind, she became ill-at-ease.

When Marielena looked as if to draw up a chair to join them, Dak pushed back from the table abruptly, rising to his feet. "If you'll excuse us, I promised Camilla a ride on the carousel before the competition," he said, taking Camilla's hand and drawing her up and away from the table.

A look of disappointment swept over Marielena's lovely features, but she flashed a quick smile up at Dak. "See you later, at the campfire?" she asked hopefully.

He nodded, moving away, holding Camilla's hand firmly on his arm, a gesture that brought a frown back to Marielena's face. Her companion spoke, and she bent to him, her black hair falling in a cloud of raven darkness to conceal her features.

Dak walked so fast, wielding his way through the crowd, that he was practically dragging Camilla who was finding it difficult, with her shorter step, to keep up with his long stride. Drawing her to the edge of the carnival grounds, he stopped, and Camilla was suddenly shaken at the look on his face when he turned to her.

"What is it, Dak?" she whispered.

His eyes flowed over her, and his mouth was drawn into a pronounced, straight line. He didn't speak.

Camilla saw his eyes, and she knew havoc lay beyond that dark blue glare, tormenting the mind she envisioned racing with activity.

"Dak," she entreated, "you're scaring me."

He thrust out an arm to embrace her, pulling

her to his chest. "Sorry," he whispered against her temple.

While her mind knew better, her heart demanded reassurance and she asked, peering timidly up at him. "Are you upset about Marielena? Did you want to be with her?"

"For God's sake, Goldilocks! Do you think I am that shallow with the mentality of a schoolboy?"

"But you changed as soon as she spoke to you. You didn't even finish your hamburger!" she added, driving home her point.

Dak gave a short laugh. "I didn't, did I? And I dragged you away from yours."

Camilla shrugged, intimating it was of little consequence and certainly not the real issue.

He looked down at her, his features serious again. "It wasn't Marielena," he said softly.

Puzzlement marked Camilla's porcelain silhouette beneath the garish colored lightbulbs overhead. "What then?" she asked softly.

"Dimitri," he muttered.

"Marielena's companion?"

Dak nodded.

"What about him? Do you know him?"

Again, he nodded. "I know him as Dennis Stanley. He's a double agent."

Camilla gasped.

"His real name is Demitri Stanislovi."

"Did he recognize you as well?" Camilla asked, trying to quell the quivering that was beginning in her insides.

"He would not know me. But it's known in a small circle within the agency who he is. They have been trying to learn his whereabouts for a long time now."

"Does a double agent mean that he works for the other side but has infiltrated your agency with the intention of being disloyal? Would he betray you without a qualm?" Camilla asked all in one breath, wanting to understand this work in which Dak was enmeshed.

"Actually, it means he is working both sides," he answered. "Whichever is the most advantageous. He would, and has, betrayed without a flicker of emotion. He has no allegiance to either side." He paused. "It also means that our suspicions are correct. We are in the right area for the arms that are being smuggled. Otherwise, why would he be here?"

"Perhaps hiding out?" she ventured.

He shook his head thoughtfully. "I don't think so."

Another thought occurred to Camilla, and she put it into words. "Does this also mean that Marielena is involved in this thing?"

Dak shook his head. "I doubt it. Though they may be using her for information that she isn't aware she is supplying. No," he said emphatically, "I think she's just playing footsie with some pretty questionable characters."

"Should we . . . you . . . be doing anything about it?"

"I'll contact Earl tonight when I get back and pass it on to him."

"If you want to go back to the castle now," Camilla offered, "we can."

Dak shook his head. "No, I want to hang around here a while. See what I can find out. Besides, I have that joust in a little while. No way to explain not showing up after I've been seen here. I cannot afford to arouse suspicions."

"Is there," she asked dubiously, "anything I can do?"

Dak smiled down on her, unable to dismiss her naive offer of help. He touched the tip of her nose with his fingertip. "Don't stick that pretty little nose into this affair, Goldilocks. It could get ugly, and I certainly don't want you involved if it does."

When she looked as if to protest, his finger slipped to her lips. "No," he said firmly. "Now, come on. Let's ride the carousel."

Sitting astride a grinning, colorful wooden horse, she asked Dak about the joust.

"Two men compete each night," he explained. "On Saturday, the last night, the winning six knights will compete against each other until there is one final winner. Part of the competition is a game of skill where one must catch the brass ring on his lance while galloping down the runway. They begin with a four-inch ring, progressing through graduated sizes down to the last one, a mere one-eighth of an inch in diameter. If you miss any one of them, you are eliminated. It is traditional for the winner to select his choice for the Queen of Love and Beauty.

"Don't Knights have names?" she asked thoughtfully.

"They do."

"What is yours?"

"The Dark Knight."

"Oh," she murmured.

A twitch of a smile played about Dak's mouth. "Disappointed?" he asked.

She frowned, shaking her head in a negative motion. "It's just that I envisioned you with a more traditional name like Sir Lancelot or Galahad." She waved her hand expressively. "You know, something that says 'gallant.' Something like Lord of Casco."

"You have too much imagination," he teased.

"Well, you do reside in a castle, and a man who lives in such a dwelling should have a more imaginative name," she said emphatically.

"I'll remember that if I ever play Knight again."

She frowned even though she knew his manner was lighthearted teasing. "You should have used Galileo," she said pensively. "That has a quaint charm about it."

"Think so?" he asked off-handed.

"Of course," she expounded. "It hints at so much more than Dark Knight. That sounds like you're the bad guy."

Dak chuckled aloud at that observation. "I meant it to be mysterious, unknown," he told her.

"Well," she drawled acquiesing. "I guess it is that, too."

"Besides, there already is a bad guy as you put it."

"There is?" She perked up.

Dak nodded. "Calls himself the Black Shadow."

"Is he your opponent?"

"Not tonight. I go up against the Green Wizard. But talk is that the Black Shadow will be one of the final contestants."

"Well, you'll beat him if he is."

Again, Dak chuckled. "You haven't seen him joust . . . or me . . . for that matter."

Camilla's mouth moved, pondering the thought. "You'll still beat him," she said decisively, offering no reason.

The carousel stopped, and Dak slid off his mount, then lifted Camilla to the platform. They crossed the fair grounds to the Renaissance Faire that made one feel they had crossed an invisible line from the garishly bright lights and whirling rides to another world of costumes and pagentry. There were serfs milling among the spectators and bosomy wenches casting flirtatious eyes at anyone who looked their way. Jesters cavorted in colorful garb, tumbling and joking with the crowd. They passed a harlequin with black mask and diamond -patterned tights and shirt. He cradled a mandolin, which he strummed with a plectrum, moving it rapidly across the strings, a motion which produced a quivering, mournful sound.

In the absence of rising curtains and dimming lights to prepare an audience, the festival producers had resorted to theatrical devices of Shakespeare's day, using trumpet blasts to gain the audience's attention. They passed by trumpeteer's presenting magicians, puppeteers, jugglers, mimes, fire eaters, stilt walkers, sword swallowers, and even a human chess game. They paused to watch ten spirited Andalusian stallions perform intricate maneuvers with rigorous precision.

Later, across the arena, they stopped again to watch as two knights struggled in hand-to-hand combat in a mock ceremony that had the crowd cheering for their favorite.

"Shall we go watch Marielena dance?"

Camilla shrugged. "If you want."

The gypsy camp was on the edge of the woods. A fortune teller's tent was set up on one side with a sign inviting those so desiring to come in and have Madame Illiana tell their fortune or read their palm. As they approached, a giggling young girl came out to join her waiting friend. Waiting her turn, a middle-aged woman hurried through the curtained doorway, eager and expectant of hearing the details of a wondrous future.

Camilla paused, studying the sign that proclaimed Madame Illiana "knows all and tells all."

Dak bent to her. "Surely you're not considering having your palm read?"

"Maybe she could tell me about my past," she said seriously.

Dak shook his head. "Forget it. I hate to be skeptical, but you have a better chance of recalling your past on your own."

She drew a resigned sigh, and they moved on.

A small knot of people had gathered round the campfire. The band of gypsy wagons, painted in bright orange, red and blues, were assembled in a semi-circle. Black-haired gypsy children ran through the clearing around the painted wagons with high spirited playfulness, while their elders read cards, offered games of chance, or sold food from the brightly lit caravans.

Dak drew Camilla to the side where in the center of the clearing, with a bonfire in the background, a man and woman were finishing their seductive dance of conquered love in the glow of the firelight. The gypsy woman's full, ruffled skirt swirled with her movements. The man circled round her, and they teased, entertaining the onlookers with provocative undulating bodies that dipped and swayed in time to the music. The man's black booted feet stamped the ground, matching the tempo of the music. Just as the crowd was thoroughly enthralled, watching with breath abated for the man to emerge triumphantly, the music died abruptly. The woman had sunk to her knees in the dust, pleading at the gypsy man's feet. The crowd applauded, and the couple took their bows, then slipped away into the darkness well beyond the firelight.

The music started again amid the mingled clatter of tambourines, a violin, and the distinct click-click of castanets. With a leap that would have rivaled any ballet dancer, Marielena landed with a swirl of orchid skirts and a flash of bare brown legs. An orchid was tucked in the deep waves of her cloud of black hair. The silken fabric of her white blouse draped her figure seductively, leaving her shoulders bare and exposing the rounded curves of her breast. Her sandaled feet moved with whisper light step across the ground. The firelight behind her played over her features, dancing erotically over her body as she tantalized the crowd with sensual, liquid movements.

She whirled. She leaped. She bent, enchanting with her eyes -- those dark, sultry eyes -- and with her legs, long, slender, enticing, and with lips as red as wine and as tastefully inviting. Her body, volumptuously curved, was evident despite the full skirts that swirled above her thighs. The tiny waist was nipped in with a bright yellow sash. Her bosom, thrust taut against the fabric of her blouse, teased, heaving with heavy breaths as she whirled. And amid it all, the black eyes searched, leaping frenetically through the crowd.

Camilla watched her. Graceful as a swan, she went through the motions of her dance. Her nimble fingers clicked the castanets rhymically, but it was all automatic. Her eyes were more alive than even the rising and falling of her heaving bosom. Those dark eyes that were searching for something -- or someone. The thought crossed Camilla's mind at the moment that Marielena located Dak in the crowd. If eyes could smile, the gypsy girl's certainly did at that moment. Camilla glanced up to see Dak's reaction. Much to her consternation, his face was unreadable. He stood quietly, a slight smile on his features, masking any emotions he may have. She glanced back at the gypsy girl.

Marielena was whirling to a frenetic click-click of castanets, circling round the inner circle created by the crowd of onlookers. Suddenly, in a flash of orchid skirts and flying yellow sash, she leaped into the crowd that separated as neatly as Moses' parting the water. Camilla had to step aside quickly to avoid the swirling skirts and long-legged movements.

Fascinated, she watched, as Marielena circled adroitly around Dak, smiling up at him through red painted lips, her hair billowing in a tousled mass. The mesmerized crowd cheered. The sound of the castanets filled the air, having the same effect on the crowd, as jungle drums that beat incessantly until it resounded in the veins of the dancers, inducing them to pick up the tempo with their stamping feet. The crowd began to applaud in time to the click of the castanets, cheering the gypsy girl on to victory in conquering the man she had singled out from the gathering.

But Camilla had seen Dak's mouth draw into a firm line, and his eyes cloud, concealing his chagrin. He was not pleased with the attention Marielena was publicly displaying with such wanton abandon, nor did he like the cat and mouse game she played at his expense. Perhaps Marielena had seen the displeased look as well, for she suddenly leaped back into the clearing, landing in a swirl of orchid and yellow.

Dak turned abruptly to Camilla. "I must go see that Rajah is ready. The competition will start soon." He took her arm leading her away from the horde of onlookers unable to mask their fascination with Marielena's performance -- both, he was aware, within the circle and without.

Dejected, Camilla fell into step beside him. They left the gypsy camp without a backward glance.

9

I met a murder on the way --
Shelley

*C*amilla stood on the sidelines of the jousting arena watching with an enthusiastic crowd that cheered riotously as Dak rode into the arena on Rajah. The white feathered plume waved jauntily with each step of the trotting movement of the horse. Dak circled round the ring once, then took his place, waiting for the Green Wizard to make his entrance.

And make an entrance, he did -- to the sound of trumpets blaring. He rode in on a white stallion draped in a lime green blanket and hood that fit snugly over its head. The Green Wizard rose in the stirrups, bowing to the ladies and saluting the gentlemen. He was attired in an outfit of the same shade of lime green, right down to his high topped boots. His helmet sported a plume, large and showy, in the exact shade of matching green. The man was theatrical, confident that his jousting skills would equal his ability to mesmerize a crowd. With prancing steps, his steed carried him back to the starting line.

Camilla flung a fleeting glance at Dak. Jousting was probably a new sport to him. After all, when had he had time to indulge in such activities? She didn't want to see him defeated and sent up a little prayer that he could match the Green Wizard's skill. She could not see his face, only the eyes peering from the slits in the helmet. Anyway, she was too far away to gauge his feelings now. However, he did sit astride Rajah in a confident manner. The blare of the trumpets sounded again, and she turned her attention back to the center of the arena.

Moments later, both horses came charging into the arena, drawing their rider closer and closer to his opponent. Lances were drawn and held firmly, ready for the thrust that would send his rival to the ground and elevate the one still seated to victory.

Dak plunged forward with his lance, but the Green Wizard fielded the blow which would have sent him plunging to earth. Both riders turned their steeds and raced back up the runway. The crowd was cheering as the two horses turned again and again, carrying their equally matched riders to meet his adversary. The stallion's hooves pounded the earth, throwing clods of dirt into the atmosphere in their hell-bent race to bring their rider to victory.

The Green Wizard thrust his lance with a direct hit, and Camilla caught her breath, covering her mouth with both hands to stifle a scream. But Dak, the Dark Knight, was not to be counted out yet. Anticipating the thrust, he rose in the saddle with his shield held firmly. It caught the glancing blow with a sound that resounded through the crowd of onlookers. They gasped in unison, one long, loud breath as they watched spellbound for the Dark Knight to fall. Their shouts turned to frenzied screaming as they saw the Dark Knight lean into the thrust with all his might behind the shield. Confident of an imminent victory, the force caught the Green Wizard off guard and sent him falling backwards off of his stallion, the lance flipping upward like a baton thrown into the air. He tumbled, feet over head, in a green ball of slow motion that held the crowd breathless as he plummeted to earth.

When he hit the ground, the crowd went wild, erupting into earth-shattering cheering. The trumpets began to blare, and the loudspeaker announced the winner of the evening as the Dark Knight.

Camilla was clapping her hands and joining in the exhilarating cheering of the crowd. She saw Dak turn, scanning the onlookers. When he located her, he touched his helmet with his fingetips and bowed slightly from where he sat astride Rajah. Camilla smiled, applauding until he left the arena and disappeared from her sight. Then she made her way through the heavy knot of people toward the stalls where Dak would take Rajah to be rubbed down.

She met him just as he had removed his helmet and cloak in preparation to rub down Rajah's glistening coat. Impulsively, she ran to him. His arms caught her in a quick embrace.

"You did it!" she exclaimed, beaming up at him.

"Luck," he replied.

She shook her head. "Shrewd," she retorted. "And," she added emphatically, "you'll beat the Black Shadow, too!"

"Thanks for the vote of confidence, but don't be too certain. This is not in my usual line of work."

"You'll still win," she said, tilting her jaw at a positive angle.

He turned her away from him, giving her a little push toward the fair grounds. "Go amuse yourself while I take care of Rajah. I won't be long," he said softly.

Camilla, peering back over her shoulder at him, felt like his eyes were smiling at her, and once again she had that sensation that those deep, blue eyes were different from the ones in her memory that haunted her. "I'll be over by the tent where Henry the VIII is selling those enormous turkey legs."

Dak grinned. "Catch up with you shortly."

Smiling, she wagged her fingertips at him as she walked away.

Strolling along nonchalantly, Camilla paused at a jewelry stand to admire the handpainted wares. She picked up a pair of earrings, and then a charm bracelet that had small, handpainted charms of knights, harlequins, horses, and other figures depicting the Renaissance Faire. Laying it back down, she turned toward the childish laughter of children at the next stand who were having their faces painted. Their happiness made her smile. Slowly, she moved away, thoughts welling in her mind about her own childhood. Where had she grown up? How? Did she have brothers or sisters? She frowned as the varied questions plagued her senses, wondering if she were ever going to regain all of those lost years. Sometimes the answers seemed so close to the surface, but when she strove to bring them forward, they always eluded her, dissipating like mist on the sea.

Camilla had wandered to the edge of the gypsy tents where Madame Illiana had offered her fortune telling skills. She looked up at the sign. What could it hurt? On impulse, her hand touched the curtain that hung over the opening of the doorway. She cast a quick look around. The area was deserted except for a small knot of people hovering near a booth offering a game of chance.

Slowly, she pulled back the curtain, peering into the dimly lit interior. As her sight had not yet fully adjusted to the interior darkness, she blinked in momentary confusion, aware of a man sprawled on the floor, and of another crossing the short expanse of the tented area toward her. Something about his manner, combined with the grimace on his dark, swarthy features, alerted her intuition with little piercing arrows of alarm.

She started to draw back, but before she could do so, the man had gained the entrance. He struck out at her, ramming her with his elbow so hard, he knocked her to the ground. Camilla screamed, for in his hand he brandished a long-bladed knife, and she would have had to be blind not to see the blood dripping from the curved blade. The man leaped over her prostrate figure and ran away, disappearing into the shadows of the perimeter of the fair grounds. A woman's scream echoed Camilla's and hurried footsteps brought several pairs of hands to her aid. The closest ones bent to help her to her feet.

"Camilla!"

She looked up, saw Dak burst through the crowd. He bent down to her. "What has happened? Are you hurt?"

Camilla's eyes sought his. "I . . . I think someone has been injured . . . maybe killed. I was thinking about going in to see the gypsy when a man came out of the tent and knocked me down. He was carrying a knife . . . a . . . a dagger. There was blood on it."

Dak rose swiftly and entered the tent. Seconds later, he pulled back the curtain, calling to a security guard striding toward them. "Call the police," he told him quietly. "We have an injured man in here."

Other security guards flocked to the area, immediately dispersing the curious onlookers. Dak pulled Camilla aside. "The police will want to question you. Did you recognize the man?"

She shook her head. "Of course not. How could I? I know no one here, except you. It all happened so fast."

Dak's frown deepened, and he shook his head.

"What is it?" she whispered, seeming to understand that Dak was aware of something that the security guards were not.

"The man inside is dead," he said quietly.

That didn't surprise her. His next words did.

"It was Dimitri."

Camilla's mouth formed a small round circle.

He put his arm around her shoulders, murmuring, "It seems our plot thickens."

92

Camilla was suddenly afraid. "What should I do? Should I tell them anything?"

Dak nodded. "Exactly what you've told me. And then we have to get out of here and back to the castle so I can contact Earl."

10

Life and the memory of it
cramped, dim . . .

A n hour later, they were on the path en route home, jogging along astride Rajah.

"You're concerned about Dimitri being murdered, aren't you?" Camilla ventured, in the wake of his silence. "You think it has something to do with the case you're working on?"

"It seems a distinct possibility."

Only moments after they had returned to the castle, the radio began to crackle and Casper's voice inquired, "Galileo? Are you there? Come in, Galileo."

Dak tossed his cloak onto a chair and hurried to receive the call. "I'm here, Earl -- "

"Where the hell have you been?" The voice demanded, interrupting his words.

Ignoring the question, Dak said, "I was just going to call you."

"Well, I've been trying to get you for hours," his friend told him, intimating he was still waiting for an answer to his question.

Dak didn't assuage his curiosity. "We've got problems," he told his partner.

"What's up?"

"Remember Dennis Stanley?"

"How could I forget the s.o.b.," Earl Babcock snapped. "I lost a very good friend because of him. Why?"

"He's dead."

"Where are you getting this information?" Babcock inquired.

"First hand. He was stabbed tonight at the Renaissance Faire."

"Holy hell! Reason?"

"Don't know yet," Dak told him. "But I'd say it's a pretty safe bet he was involved in this arms deal."

"Got anything else on that?"

"Not yet. Still watching." Dak words were frustrated. "I see no signs of any smuggling in the bay."

"Well, stay with it for a while," Earl said. There was a slight pause, then quietly, "Dak?"

The hesitant tones, and his use of Dak, alerted him to the sincerity of his partner's voice and a prescience of what was to come.

"Yes?"

"Goldilocks? I presume she's still there?"

Dak's eyes met Camilla's. "Yes. She is. Why?" He didn't have to ask the question. His gut was telling him that Earl had learned Camilla's past.

"She is the daughter of Jonathan K. Lloyd, a wealthy businessman. He died about two years ago of a heart attack en route from Europe."

Dak's eyes were on Camilla. He saw her sink onto the nearest seat in front of the fireplace, and he saw the green eyes cloud when she heard her father was dead. The marble gargoyles behind her stared out solemnly, casting a stony-eyed gaze across her shoulder.

"Other family?" Dak asked quietly.

"None. Her mother died years ago when she was just a child. She lives alone. There is, however, a boyfriend. A Dr. Branson Phillips."

Camilla's head had dropped to her hands.

"Have you nothing to say?" Earl demanded.

"What would you like me to say?"

"She is on the missing person's list," Earl told him quietly and when there was still no response, he exclaimed, "For God's sake, Dak! You could be charged with kidnapping! Her boyfriend has been searching all over for her. They're engaged."

Dak ignored that last remark, saying, "Don't worry about the kidnapping charge, Moth. I did not keep her here against her will. She will vouch for that." His eyes swung to look at Camilla again, but her face was still buried in her hands. "Have you contacted the boyfriend?"

"No. That's for you to do. Got a pen and paper?"

Dak reached for a note pad and scribbled down the phone number that Casper gave him.

"You will call him?" was asked dubiously over the crackle of the radio.

"Yes," Dak replied quietly. "I'll see that she contacts him."

"Try to get this thing settled, will you? We can't afford to have it jeopardize our initial purpose."

"I know," Dak replied quietly.

"It seems Goldilocks and her doctor boyfriend quarreled. She ran off in anger. My sources tell me the poor guy has been frantic trying to find her."

"I'll have her call him first thing in the morning."

"Tonight."

"No," Dak said firmly. "It's too late, and she needs time to adjust. We'll contact him tomorrow."

"All right," Earl conceded with a sigh.

Dak changed the subject. "Any further developments here with Dimitri Stanislovi, or anything else, and I'll call you."

"Good," Earl repeated. "I'll be waiting to hear from you."

The line went dead, and Dak turned his attention to Camilla. He strode across the floor and bent down to her where she still sat with her head in her hands. Gently, he pulled her hands away from her face.

Her green eyes were stricken. "I have no family," she said solemnly. "There really is no one who cares." Her words confirmed her suspicions, and the fears that had been goading her heart with little piercing arrows of unconscious awareness.

"You have a boyfriend," Dak replied quietly.

"We quarreled."

Dak shrugged. "Lover's quarrel. Everyone has them."

She shook her head. "I don't think so." She waggled her fingers before him. "He said we were engaged, but I have no ring. It must have been serious."

"It can be patched up," he said, avoiding her

eyes.

Camilla pulled away one hand to grasp his jaw and make him look at her. "I don't feel like the same person that was engaged to this man," she whispered, her words fevered with panic. "I don't feel any love in my heart for him . . . and I should, shouldn't I, if I loved him enough to accept his ring? Surely, my heart would remember even if my mind doesn't."

Dak was cognizant of the green eyes filling and the lower lip beginning to tremble and knew she was very close to tears. "Take it slowly, Goldilocks," he said gently. "This has all hit you quite suddenly. Don't rush it, or let it rush you. It will all come back in time . . . even the feelings."

"I feel ambushed with all the crazy thoughts . . . the doubts -- " she faltered.

"That's natural, I would assume," he said, brushing back her hair from her forehead. "Tomorrow when you see him, even if you don't remember fully, your heart will let you reach out to him." He winked at her trying for a bit of lightheartedness. "When it truly loves, hearts don't forget," he said softly.

But Camilla didn't smile. Instead she squeaked. "Tomorrow? I have to see him tomorrow?"

"You can't put it off, Goldilocks. You must face him and your fears."

"And blue eyes," she murmured.

"Are his eyes blue?" he asked with a quirk of his eyebrow.

She shrugged. "I don't know, but they must be, otherwise why would I feel so sad about them?"

Dak had no answer for that. "Well," he said cheerfully, "you are obviously very rich." But even that revelation brought her no consolation, and he rose, drawing her up from the chair. "Come over here. I have something for you."

He pulled her to the chair where he had flung his cloak, rummaged in the pocket, and withdrew a small tissue wrapped package. He handed it to her. "Sorry it isn't more elegantly wrapped," he said.

Her eyes questioned him. "What is it?"

"Open it."

She unwrapped the tissue paper slowly, her eyes flicking from him to the tiny parcel in her hand. Nestled in her palm was the charm bracelet she had admired at the fair. Her finger touched one of the tiny, gold-plated knights. "Oh, Dak! I saw this tonight and liked it. How did you know?" She held out her wrist for him to clasp it for her.

"I didn't," he admitted, hooking the tiny gold circle. "It's just a little trinket of no real value, but I wanted you to have a momento from the fair and . . . and --" he faltered, something that was foreign to his nature. "I wanted you to remember the time we've spent together."

Camilla flung herself into his arms. "How could I ever forget these past two days," she murmured. "They have been like a lifetime . . . and a lifeline. I love the bracelet, Dak. I'll treasure it, and I want you to know, I'll never forget you, never. After I call Bran . . . Branson," she stumbled over the name, "tomorrow, I know I must go back home, to another life. But we still have until Saturday." She peered up at him. "You do want me to stay until the jousting match, don't you?"

"I'd be disappointed if you didn't," he said softly.

She clung to him silently, and he held her,

his lips brushing against her golden hair. When he held her back from him, he asked, "Are you hungry? I did drag you away from your burger."

Before she could answer, his hand slid down her arm to clasp her hand, and he headed to the kitchen, pulling her along. "How about some eggs? I make great eggs benedict."

11

The day shall not be up so soon as I,
To try the fair adventure of tomorrow.
Shakespeare

*I*n the very darkest time of the night, Camilla rose, awakened from a light and fitful sleep by thoughts that would not stop nagging at her. Much as she had the first night she had arrived, she stood at the long window, looking out into the inky blackness of those hours after midnight. She shivered. Tomorrow terrified her. Meeting this doctor -- Branson Phillips -- terrified her. She didn't know where she stood with him or that other life. How serious was their quarrel? Did she still love him? If so, why had she run away to Maine, to a place where he had not been able to find her?

And her heart whispered of a new dilemma . . . did she even still want to be in love with him? Somehow she felt changed. Maybe not outwardly, but certainly inwardly. Was it Dak?

Had he made her see life from a new perspective? Perhaps, she had not been in love with Branson Phillips at all. Her frown deepened, and a great sigh escaped her. A feeling deep within her soul mocked her, making her aware in her heart, that she had, indeed, once loved this man named Branson. That she couldn't remember him, or that love, plagued her. What had gone so wrong? Another sigh dragged up from the lower regions of her stomach, concealing Dak's footsteps as he approached her sprite-like figure, standing in the white poet shirt, ghostlike in the shadows of the castle.

Though she didn't hear him, she was intuitive of his approach and didn't turn around. Silently, he rested his hands on her shoulders, and she drew comfort from his nearness and his touch. Camilla raised her hands to cover his.

"Can't sleep?" he murmured.

She shook her head. Dak sensed the turmoil she was feeling, and they stood silently for a very long time. Finally, he led her back to the bed, pulled back the covers, and motioned for her to get in. Without a word, she did so. Gently, he pulled the covers up over her. "Try not to worry about tomorrow, Goldilocks," he said softly.

"I can't help it." She suddenly reached up, catching at his hand. "I don't want to be alone when I see him."

Dak sighed and sat down on the bed beside her. "Tell you what, Goldilocks, we'll call him in the morning and arrange a meeting here. I'll be around if you need me."

Camilla held his hand to the porcelain whiteness of her cheek. "Thank you, Dak," she whispered.

"By the way, " he said seriously, "after you see him, things . . . your feelings . . . may change. If that happens and you want to leave with him, I don't want you to feel any obligation to stay for the joust." His eyes held hers and he sensed a moment of protest. "Promise?" he demanded.

Not thinking that likely, she smiled. "Promise."

"Do you think you can sleep now?" he asked.

"Maybe."

"Then let me give you something else to think about." He leaned down toward her. "How would you like to go on a picnic tomorrow?"

Camilla bobbed up in the bed. "A picnic! But how? Don't I have to meet Branson tomorrow?"

"We'll call first thing in the morning. Arrange your meeting for late afternoon. That will give us plenty of time for a picnic." He pressed her back down among the pillows. "I have a wonderful, mysterious place to show you."

"Where?"

He shook his head. "Not until tomorrow. It's a surprise." He paused, asking in afterthought. "I don't suppose you packed a swimsuit?" he asked jovially.

"Certainly!" she laughed. "It's with all my other clothes in a suitcase in a car parked God know's where! And there's nothing that even remotely resembles a swimsuit in my attic box. Trust me, I've been through everything."

"Never mind. We'll think of something."

"Dak, where on earth would we swim now? A motel with an indoor pool?"

Again, he shook his head. "Not until

tomorrow. I told you, it's a surprise." He bent forward, brushing her forehead with a brief kiss. "Now close your eyes and explore your imagination for the magic of fantasies that dreams are made of."

She moved her head from side to side. "You are so enigmatic. So reserved, full of strength and courage one moment, and the next talking of fantasy and magic."

"All work and no play makes Dak a dull boy," he tossed blithely at her.

She laughed.

He rose.

"Good night," he said softly.

"Good night," she whispered.

12

*C*amilla awoke the next morning feeling dewy from the realms of a dream that left her expectant of the day's outing. She stretched languidly, peering over at the corner where Dak's bedroll should have been. But it had been rolled up and put away, and hurriedly she pushed back the covers and swung her legs over the edge of the bed.

Dak came from the kitchen, greeting her cheerfully, "Good morning, Goldilocks. Sleep well, I hope?"

"Yes. Why didn't you wake me?"

"Wasn't necessary. You needed to rest."

"I'll get a quick bath and then help you pack the picnic."

"Too late. That's done," he said. He held

up his hand, silencing the apology. "No matter. Now scoot and get your bath." He held her eyes for a moment. "Then we'll make your call."

She nodded agreeably, but he saw the dread push away the light that had been in the green eyes when she had wakened. He turned back to the kitchen. It couldn't be helped. She had to face this bugaboo, like it or not. And that included himself, he thought dryly.

When Camilla came from her bath, she wore the white Victorian dress, only this time she was not nude beneath it, having rinsed out her lingerie before she'd gone to bed. Instead of her high heeled shoes, she opted for the low heeled sandals. She ran her fingers through her still damp hair, surveying Dak from where she stood.

His mouth drew up at the corner, and his eyes took on a strange look as they flowed over her thoughtfully. "I love the way you look in that, but it's a bit dressy for where we're going."

She spread her hands expressively. "I have nothing else."

"I know. You just look as delicate as a rose," he murmured. "I feel like I should be escorting you to a cotillion, rather than to -- " He let his words trail off into nothing, then asked spritely, "How about some breakfast?"

She shook her head. "Let's call first. I'm so nervous, I don't think I could eat a bite."

"Would you like me to talk to him first?"

She smiled thinly. "Yes . . . ," she admitted with a nod of her head, "but I can't let you. I have to do this myself."

He smiled encouragingly, with a nod. "Ready?"

"Ready," she murmured, watching Dak as

he put the call through.

When he had Branson Phillips on the line, Dak handed the receiver over to her.

"Branson? This is Camilla." Her heart was pounding so hard, she felt like it was strangling her words.

"Camilla? My God, Camilla! Where are you? I have been worried sick."

"Branson, please, listen to me a minute. I was hit by a tree limb during a storm, and I . . . I don't remember much of anything that happened before that. In fact, I . . . I don't remember you."

"What the hell do you mean, you don't remember me?" he demanded.

"Just as I said. I seem to be suffering from amnesia."

"Amnesia!" He was silent a moment, then asked skeptically, "Are you leveling with me? This is not some crazy joke, is it?"

"No joke," she replied quietly.

She heard him exhale in one long breath.

"Where are you?" he asked.

"I'm in Maine."

"Give me directions. I'll come get you."

"Branson," she said softly, "I am aware that you and I quarreled. I don't know why or what about, but I am not going back with you. Not just yet. I am going to stay here a couple more days --"

He interrupted her. "Camilla, I need to see you. Please. I love you. Let me explain."

"I agree, we need to talk, but I need some time. I'll tell you where I am if you'll promise not to badger me. I need to get myself in control again. Will you agree to that?"

"Yes. Of course. Just please, tell me where you are? I'll leave right now."

"No. I'll meet with you at three o'clock --"

"Why?" he interrupted her again. "Why do you want me to wait?"

"Branson," she felt the pleading in her voice. "Please do as I ask."

She heard him sigh deeply before acquiescing. "All right. Give me the address."

Camilla handed the receiver to Dak. Abruptly, she strode across the room, thrust open the door, and went outside into the fresh air. She plopped down on the stone step, hugging her arms about her, and feeling a rolling in her stomach that was making her ill.

It was not long before Dak joined her. Without a word, he handed her a mug of coffee, and sat down beside her.

She sipped her coffee in silence. And he said nothing.

When her coffee was gone, he stood up, taking her cup from her hands. "Let's go where it's quiet, where the cares of the world are left behind."

"I know of no such place," she said.

"Well, I do. Come on." He hooked the cup handles over one finger of his left hand and took her hand with the other, pulling her to her feet.

She followed him through the kitchen where he put the cups in the sink, picked up a wicker basket, which she presumed held their picnic lunch, and a small canvas bag. He handed the canvas bag to Camilla and picked up a kerosene lantern. She looked at him with questioning eyes, but he only smiled, giving no explanation, and opened the kitchen door, stepping aside for her to precede him. He followed, closing the door behind them.

"Come on. This way," he directed, crossing the back yard beyond the stable to the wooded area.

She followed his footsteps until they came to a craggy cliffside overlooking the bay. It was a wonderful view, the sun was shining, and it was peaceful, so she asked, "Is this where we're having our picnic?"

He shook his head, pointing. She followed his pointing finger. Among the craggy rocks, tucked into the crevice of the stone was what appeared to be an opening. "A cave? You want me to go into a cave?" She shook her head. "I don't think so. Much as I like your company, I'm afraid of what may be in there."

He laughed. "Probably only a few bats."

She looked repulsed, and he chuckled again.

"What about bears?" she asked.

"Bears aren't going to bother you, Goldilocks," he retorted good-naturedly.

She rolled her eyes.

He held out his hand to her. "If you'll come with me, I promise you won't be disappointed. Didn't I tell you last night I have a surprise for you?"

She placed her hand in his. "This better be good," she said, with pseudo-sternness.

He chuckled as they started the descent up the rocky path to the yawning dark crevice spliced eons ago into the cliffside. At the narrow, dark opening, they entered. Dak's footsteps were surer than hers. She moved with trepidation, easing into the darkness, casting a wary look around as he paused to light the lantern.

Following his footsteps, they went deeper and deeper into the cavern. Finally able to contain herself no longer, she asked, "Where on earth are we going?"

"Are you tired?" he inquired, turning back to her.

"No, but aren't you afraid we'll get lost? We've taken so many turns."

"Don't worry," he assured her. "I've been here many times. It's not far now."

"What's not far?"

"Our picnic grounds."

She frowned, and he chuckled again. "Smile, Goldilocks, we're about to embark on a glorious adventure."

"It had better be," she mumbled. And heard him chuckle again.

Some time later, he turned back to her. "There's a little crawl space we have to get through. Can you manage?" He indicated a small, oval opening in the glow of the lantern light.

Surveying the rather skinny hole, Camilla's eyes grew wide. "Are you serious?"

In answer, he shoved the wicker basket through to the other side, then reached up for the canvas bag she held. It followed the basket, and then Dak disappeared. Camilla felt a moment's panic. Then Dak poked his head back through the opening. He sported a big grin. "Ready?"

"As I'll ever be," she moaned, bending to reach his outstretched arm thrust into the opening to assist her.

On the other side, Camilla stood speechless, gazing through the murky light of the lantern at the cavernous space before her. Gray rock walls surrounded a pool of water so clear she knew she would be able to see the bottom should she venture close enough. Her fascinated gaze was drawn upward by the sound of rushing water. Dak held the lantern light high. She caught her breath. Cascading from the rock wall, high above the glistening pool of water was a waterfall. In the scintillating glow of the lamplight, the surface of the cascade rippled, creating tiny droplets that glistened like jewels dancing in the sunlight.

"Oh, Dak," she whispered. "This is beautiful, but utterly amazing."

"Here, hold the lantern a minute while I light a torch." He held a lighter to the long-handled torch and shoved it into a metal holder nailed into the stone wall.

"It gives the appearance of moonlight," she said softly.

"You've been a good sport, trudging along into God knows what without question, and after all," he flung his arm around her shoulders, "I did promise you a surprise."

"An understatement," she said, turning in his arms. "How ever did you find this?"

He shrugged. "Exploring. It was pretty boring up here until you came." He pulled away from the look that sprang to her eyes, continuing, "Actually, there are many caverns and underground pools all along this coast. Nobody pays much attention to them. I found this one quite by accident."

"By accident?" she parroted.

He nodded. "Swimming one day in the bay. You can get here from the bayside. One day, I decided to check out the cave and see if they were connecting. As you can see, they were."

"Weren't you afraid you'd get lost?"

"I have been trained to get in and out of many kinds of places. It's a skill one acquires in my business," he replied in an off-handed way. He picked up the wicker basket and strode forward, setting the lantern on a protruding flat rock, then swung the picnic basket up beside it. Camilla followed him, bringing the canvas bag. She stood idly, surveying the pool.

"Now I know why you asked if I had packed a swimsuit." She sighed. "I do wish I had."

"Not to worry," he said, taking the canvas bag from her. He flicked the zipper with a quick motion and rummaged inside. "I thought this might do," he said casually, dropping the bag and holding out the poet shirt she had worn the past two nights to sleep in.

Her green eyes went round. "Surely you don't mean I could use that to swim in?" Her words were aghast.

Indignation had settled on his mouth, and that glowering look leaped to his eyes. It was that same look she had seen that first night when she had angered him with her distrust.

"Camilla," he began softly, "surely we have come beyond this." His voice rose. "We've been sleeping in the same room for God's sake! If I wanted to take advantage of you, I could certainly have done so before now. There has been ample opportunity."

And she was suddenly abashed. "You're right. I'm sorry," she murmured.

His sigh was heavy. "Haven't you learned by now you can trust me?"

She took a step closer to him. "I'm sorry, Dak. It's not you. I . . . I think it's me. Actually," she admitted softly, "I'm not sure what kind of person I was in that other life. Maybe . . . maybe I'm more afraid of myself than I am you." She took the shirt from his hand. "This was thoughtful of you. Of course, I'll wear it. Did you bring swim trunks?"

He nodded.

She stretched up on tip-toe and kissed his cheek. "Please, don't let me spoil this wonderful surprise. Come on. Let's go swimming," she whispered winsomely.

After a slow, measuring look, he gave her a smiling nod, dismissing the awkward moment. "You can go over behind that rock to change. I'll wait here."

Camilla went behind the rock, removed the Victorian dress, and her bra. Her panties, a mere wisp of silk and lace, would take no time to dry, and so she left them on. She slipped into the poet shirt, smiling to herself remembering the first time she had worn it. Buttoning the front, her fingers were lost among the ruffles. Minutes later, she came out from behind the concealing rock, carrying her clothing.

"Cute," Dak said nonchalantly. "I like that on you."

"Yeah, I just might start a whole new fashion with the way I've been dressing these past few days."

Dak chuckled as he caught up his swim trunks and headed toward the concealment of the gray rock.

While he disappeared behind the rock, she folded her clothes and placed them on the rock beside their lunch basket.

Dak emerged wearing navy blue swim trunks, tossed his bundle of rolled up clothing to the top of the rock, and caught up her hand. "Let's go test the water," he invited.

The water was cool, but they disregarded it,

allowing the invigorating, clear water to wash blissfully over their bodies. They swam for a long time. Later, they sat on a light plaid blanket, and talked easily, casually about anything and everything. Dak rose. "You haven't had any breakfast. How about some lunch now?"

"I'd love it," she responded enthusiastically, jumping to her feet. "Let me help."

They spread out the lunch in the center of the blanket and sat cross-legged across from each other. Dak had made chicken salad, accompanied by small sesame rolls. There was a triangle of cheese and round crackers, a chilled bottle of Chardonnay, and a container of fresh strawberries. From inside the canvas bag, Dak produced a small brass candlestand and a candle, which he placed in the center of their picnic fare, withdrew the lighter again and lit it with a smile.

"Well," Camilla said, "you have thought of everything, haven't you?"

He winked broadly, spreading the chicken salad onto a roll and handing it to her.

Camilla bit into the roll that was soft and tasted freshly made. "This is wonderful," she commented. "They taste homemade."

Dak's head moved up and down in agreement. "Aren't they great? Marielena brought them from the village bakery early this morning. She brings me fresh baked goods and fruit once or twice a week," Dak told her, leaning over to hand her a glass of the Chardonnay.

Camilla accepted the wine in silence. She really didn't want to discuss Marielena right now.

He poured his own and raised his glass.

Camilla lifted hers, touching it slightly to his.

"To you and your future," Dak said quietly.

"And to you for helping me regain that future," she said in a subdued voice.

The glasses clinked softly in the muted lighting of their surroundings.

When their meal was done and everything was put away but the wine, they sat together on the bank overlooking the pool.

Noting her pensive look, Dak asked, "What are you thinking?"

"About that waterfall," she responded. "What do you suppose is behind it?"

"Just a rock wall. I've already looked. Want to go see?" he asked.

She nodded her head, setting aside the wine glass, and took his hand. He pulled her to her feet, and they ran to the edge and dove in. She followed Dak as he swam to the far side of the waterfall.

He flipped over, floating on his back. "Careful when you get closer," he shouted over the roaring sound of the fall. "There is a ledge, and it will be slippery."

Dak climbed onto the ledge and reached down to help Camilla. The spray of the fall peppered them with a stinging force, and she squealed, turning to shield herself against Dak. Edging along the side, they reached the sheer sweep of water poised before them like a giant crystal wall. The noise was thunderous. Dak took her hand, then disappeared through the wall of water. As she stepped through the shimmering curtain, the sheer force of the cascading water would have toppled her slight figure had Dak not had a firm hold on her. A small scream bubbled past her lips as she steadied her footing, standing next to him on a foot-wide ledge that was as slippery as glass and cold as ice. They flattened themselves against the cold, wet wall behind them. The water pounded over the top, creating a glimmering blue-white shower that slid in a roaring, perpendicular tide in front of them.

Camilla shivered. It was awesome, and it was dangerous, and she reached out to Dak. He motioned that they must go back. He edged in front of her, keeping a firm hold until they had cleared the wall of water.

When they were beyond the waterfall, he shouted, "Jump!" and she nodded, diving into the pool right behind him. When they reached the bank, Camilla was shivering uncontrollably. Cradling her arms around her , she sank onto the blanket. The poet shirt clung to her figure like a second skin. Dak dragged a towel out of the canvas bag before he dropped down beside her, drawing her into his arms. He wrapped the towel around her, holding her until the trembling stopped.

"That was nuts," he muttered. "You're freezing."

"No. I'll be all right," she retorted. "It was great! I've never seen anything so incredible. But that rock wall was freezing!" She shivered again. "It is amazing to think there is something so phenomenal down under the ground."

Dak began to rub her body rapidly, restoring the warmth to her cold limbs. He brushed a corner of the towel over her face, drying away small droplets of water. "Are you sure you're all right?" he asked.

"Of course. I'm not fragile."

"You seem as delicate as spun sugar," he said softly.

Camilla looked up at his words. Little beads

of moisture clung to his forehead, and she lifted an edge of the towel to dab at them.

The contact was magnetic, drawing her wet-shirted body to his wet, bare chest. His arms closed around her, and his lips began a trail over her neck, face, shoulders, and lips. Camilla's arms locked around his neck. She seemed lost in his touch, lost in a world where there was no one but them. Their heavy breathing hovered in the atmosphere, mingling with the crashing of the waterfall. The rumbling she felt racing in her veins coincided with the roaring that came from the cascade of the waterfall, but she could not tell where one stopped and the other began.

Dak's hands had found their way beneath the clinging fabric of the poet shirt. With tender, exploring movements, his fingers moved from her naked breasts, over her rib cage with feather lightness, and down across the soft pillow of her stomach. Without conscious thought, he pressed her backward. Just as every sense in her being was streaking to meet his passion, Dak moved abruptly, setting her aside from him. His breath came in sharp, little gasps.

Camilla, feeling bereft of the warmth of his body, reached up to him, whispering, "It's all right."

But he shook his head. "No," he said firmly.

Puzzlement clouded her features.

"Not like this, Goldilocks." He ran his fingers through his wet hair, trying to avoid contact with her. "If you knew who you were, what you had left behind, it would be different. Later, you may have regrets." His eyes held hers for a lengthy interim. "I would not want you to ever regret anything you did with me," he said

117

solemnly.

A pulse beat in Camilla's throat, rendering her momentarily silent, despite fervid emotions that pounded, demanding a conclusion. She sat up, her fingers working with absent-minded movements at the buttons on the poet shirt. Her blond head moved from side to side, and she stood up abruptly, turning her back to him. He saw her rub her hands over her face, and then with a quick movement, removed the silk and lace wisp beneath the poet shirt. She turned back to him, the poet shirt draping her breasts seductively, still clung damply to her body.

"This . . . this seems so right," she whispered. "Don't take this moment away from us, Dak. Soon I must leave you and return to that other life." She held out her hands in a beseeching movement, and he reached out to clasp them. "Make love to me, Dak," she whispered earnestly. "Please."

The next moment, she was in his arms again, and then his body covered hers. He crooned her name over and over. Camilla arched her body against him. She seemed to be drowning in a pool of desire that she had no memory of ever sensing before. And as his desire grew, matching hers, she suddenly lay taut, straining, her body rigid, and not complying with her demands.

Dak paused mid-thrust, noting her face was set firmly, her eyes were squeezed tightly shut, and her mouth was drawn into a grim line. Abruptly, he rolled to the side.

Camilla's eyes blinked open. "What's the matter?" she whispered.

Dak stared up at the gray cavern ceiling, trying to still the tumultuous havoc in his body.

"Unless I miss my guess, I'd say you're a virgin."

"I am?" she breathed.

"'Fraid so, Goldilocks."

She flung herself on top of him. "Oh, Dak! That's wonderful! I was so afraid I'd been easy in that other life. I had these crazy feelings . . . not just crazy . . . unbridled, sensual feelings! Whenever you popped into my thoughts, I engaged in the wildest fantasies," she declared all in a rush. "I didn't know if that was normal or not. Having been engaged and all, I just assumed -- Her words trailed off, and she lay there looking down on him.

His words were blunt. "If you intend to stay that way, Goldilocks, you'd better get dressed. I've just about used up all my reserve."

"Oh, oh," she faltered, casting a quick glance downward, to where she could feel the heat of his passion throbbing with an intense firmness against her thigh. "Oh, my gosh! I guess . . . this is not really fair to you," she stammered. "I mean, I did beg you to . . . to . . . "

"Get dressed, Goldilocks!" he demanded through clenched teeth, sliding her off from where she straddled him in a highly arousing position.

And clutching her clothing, she slipped behind the massive rock, though this bit of propriety seemed rather ludicrous at this point. While she dressed behind the camouflage of the lump of granite, she heard an enormous splash and peering around the rock, saw a wide circle forming in the pool where Dak had suddenly dived into the cold water.

13

Better by far you should forget and smile
Than that you should remember and be sad.

Rossetti

*I*t was nearly three o'clock, and Camilla was nervously pacing back and forth across the room. Her white sandaled feet moved with whispering treads across the tiled floor. The skirt of the Victorian dress swirled every time she reached one end of the room and turned abruptly to begin the restless retracing of her steps.

The sound of a car in the drive was audible to them both. Camilla met Dak's glance only briefly and strode resolutely to the door. As her hand rested on the knob, Dak called out her name softly. She turned.

"I'm here if you need me."

She nodded and slipped out the door.

With heart pounding, she stood in the courtyard watching as the car, a dark green

Jaguar, braked. She could see a figure through the windshield. Moments later, the car door opened and a tall, slender man got out. Handsomely attired in gray slacks, pin-striped shirt, and navy blazer, his face broke into a huge smile when he saw her. He flung the door shut hastily.

"Camilla!" he called, hurrying toward her.

He closed the gap with a few long strides, and his outstretched arms gathered her into an embrace that she endured like a statue. The coldness was difficult to ignore. He held her back from him.

Quietly, he said, "Let's sit down. We have to talk."

They sat down on the nearest garden bench, and a great sigh escaped from her.

"Camilla, please, look at me."

She turned slowly, her green eyes flowing over him. They came to rest on eyes as blue as a summer sky, and he smiled. A smile her heart remembered. It was then that something happened to Camilla. Though she was conscious of his lips moving, she did not hear, did not comprehend any of his words. Her mind was running backwards, like a reel gone haywire. She could see pictures flashing like a film clip on a movie screen. And though it only took seconds, she glimpsed her life in those flashbacks, glimpsed in one swift movement, all the joys and all the heartaches.

She raised her eyes to meet his, and the blue eyes that stared back brought tears to her own.

"You've remembered me, haven't you?" he breathed, reaching out to take her into his arms.

"Don't, Branson," she whispered, and was surprised at how easily his name came to her lips.

"You do remember, don't you?" he asked.

She nodded, but her eyes were still dull. "I remember," she repeated. "Everything."

"Camilla, you must let me explain," he began.

"Go ahead, Branson," she said quietly. "Explain the betrayal, the trust I had in you that you tossed aside without one iota of concern for me?"

"No, Camilla, it wasn't like that," he protested. He drew a heavy sigh, frowning, then with a firm set to his mouth, he said, "I was wrong. I apologize for hurting you. But, Camilla, we had a lot of good times, please don't let that one mistake destroy it. I love you."

She was silent, turning away from his beseeching words and hands.

"Don't do this, Camilla," he pleaded fervently. "Please, come back home with me. We can work this out."

Her eyes raked over him in an all enveloping look that brought a chill to his heart. "Camilla," he whispered, "I can't bear for you to look at me like that."

"Like what?"

"So . . . so dead. Like you're not really seeing me clearly."

"Oh, I see you, Branson," she whispered, "very clearly. Perhaps," she added, staring out across the courtyard, "for the first time."

He took her arms firmly, forcing her to look at him. "I'm not going to lose you, Camilla," he said adamantly. "I'm not going to let you slip away."

Camilla's eyes searched his face. "I don't think I'm that same girl that ran away from you,

Branson," she said quietly. "In ways I don't understand myself --," she said emphatically, "but I have changed."

"No," he shook his head. "You're still angry. I understand that, and I accept it. But I can't let you walk away from me. I'll make it up to you, I promise," he pleaded. "Just come back home."

"Not yet," she said quietly. "I'm not leaving until Sunday."

"Why?"

"Because I want to stay. I'm going to the jousting match with Dak."

"No."

"Yes."

"Well, you're certainly not going to continue to stay here," he snapped with a frustrated hand waving toward the castle.

She turned to him, eyes questioning.

"Come on, Camilla," he blurted. "I'm surprised you've even stayed here in this derelict rock pile with him for this long."

"Mr. Brewster has been very kind to me -- "

"Well, that's nice," he interrupted, clearly perturbed, "but it is still no reason to continue -- " He stopped abruptly, his eyes searching her face. "Is there something going on here I should know about?"

"Like what, Branson," she snapped, "one of the seamy little affairs you indulge in?"

He glared at her. "I don't like this, Camilla. It is not like you. For God's sake! You won't even let me touch you, and now you're spending the night with some man you barely know. I demand that you return with me."

Camilla stood up, refusing to defend her

relationship with Dak. "I said I will return on Sunday." She folded her arms across her breast, saying quietly, "I think you should go now." Her eyes were brimming with unshed tears.

Branson rose from the garden bench as well. A great sigh accompanied his words. He made a valiant effort to mask his agitation. "I know you are angry with me. I want to make this hurt up to you, if you will just let me." He drew her close to him, giving her a brief hug, and dropping a kiss on her forehead. "I will see you Sunday," he said firmly, striding away.

"Goodbye, Branson," she whispered over a tightening in her throat that threatened to choke her.

He turned back. "This is not over, Camilla. I won't let it be."

But it was over. She knew it; her heart knew it. Eventually, Branson would also know it. There was nothing left in their relationship to hold them together. Solemnly, she watched him get into the car, watched as he turned the car around to face the brown ribbon driveway, even returned a sad little flutter in response to his wave. She felt lost, alone like she had never been in her life.

She stood watching until the car disappeared from her sight. Then as though the rigidity had seeped from her body without warning, she sank onto the garden seat. Tears rolled down the porcelain whiteness of her cheeks. She felt like she cried not just for Branson and their lost love, but for her mother and father, for all that had gone before, and all that she must now face alone, with no one to care. And for that other life, which she had finally remembered, that now seemed empty and vaporous as sea mist.

She saw the tips of Dak's shoes in front of

her before she heard him approach. She looked up, meeting his eyes. The silent tears streaming down her face, without the audible sound of crying, struck a chord of empathy in Dak that left him winded. He knew by the stark look on her face and the ensuing emotions that she had recovered her memory. He sat down next to her, and without a word, she turned into his chest and wept.

14

All night has the casement jassamine stirred
To the dancers dancing in tune;
Till a silence fell with the waking bird,
And a hush with the setting moon.

Tennyson

The castle was silent. From the long
window across from the bed, Camilla could see a
full, luminous moon against the indigo blue of the
evening sky. It glowed brightly, lighting up the
dark corner of the room. It seemed large and close
enough to touch. She listened for the sounds of
Dak's steady breathing that would tell her he was
asleep. Slowly, she pushed back the covers
and slipped her feet into her sandals lying beside
the bed. Moving on tip-toe, she crossed the room,
held her breath as she slid back the bolt, and turned
the doorknob cautiously. Slowly, she eased the
door open, heard a squeak and cringed, turning
toward the bed roll to see if the noise had roused

Dak. The even breathing continued, and she pulled the door open just wide enough to slip through, leaving it slightly ajar for her return.

She strode out into the courtyard, her arms folded over her breast and clasping her upper arms, she stared up into the moon filled sky. A quiet peace surrounded the courtyard, encompassing the gray castle behind her that stood sentinel over its domain. Camilla drew a deep breath. How strange to remember Branson and their relationship and then to realize that it was all past tense. Was love so fragile that it could change in a matter of moments? With the slightest provocation? She must go back Sunday, just as she'd told Branson she would. It would not be easy, getting Branson out of her life. She was very much aware that he would not give up so easily.

The first of the week, she would meet with her father's partner and immerse herself in his business. Having just completed her business degree, she had planned to join her father's firm anyway. She would make a new life for herself, carving a career in her father's world. She would be fine, just fine.

Dak lay unstirring for some moments, allowing Camilla sufficient time to exit the castle. He rose, pulling on jeans, and slipping bare feet into loafers. He strode to the window nearest her bed. The moonlight cast a brilliant beam, making it easy for him to see her standing in the courtyard. With her recovered memory, they had gone to Cromwell Road and found her car just as she had left it with the suitcase flung hastily inside the trunk. It had taken only minutes for him to get it started, and they had brought it back to the castle.

Tonight, Camilla wore a white silken gown

she had packed in her suitcase. It fluttered around her slender form, teased by the coy fingers of the night breeze. She looked like a golden-haired angel, who had floated to earth to tempt him, make him question his work -- and his life.

He liked the way the gown moved seductively around her figure and thought she looked like a moon maiden, but somehow the gown didn't make her seem as vulnerable as the poet shirt. He fought to silence a deep sigh dragging up from deep inside him and shook his head pensively. Nothing would ever tug at his heart like seeing Camilla engulfed in his poet shirt.

He watched her, wondering what she was thinking. She had been so quiet after Branson left, avoiding the subject, and seeming even less willing to discuss any phase of it. He drew a deep sigh. One thing she had been firm about was leaving on Sunday. He didn't like to think of that time when she would be gone, out of his life forever. He had no right to expect otherwise. What could he offer a girl like Camilla? While he was comfortable, though certainly not wealthy, as she apparently was, she did not seem the type to be drawn to a man for his financial report. The thing that nagged at him the most was his career that had proven to be a strain on matrimonial strings, proving over and over its unkindness to marriage. Also to be reckoned with was the age difference. He probably seemed a father figure to her.

Dak scowled. He turned abruptly. He must be getting soft in his old age, he chastised silently. Might as well enjoy himself for the rest of her stay. What the hell! He had nothing to lose. He strode over and put his favorite record on the old turntable, flipped the *on* knob and proceeded out of the room, leaving the door wide open behind him.

He moved across the stone patio with whisper light footsteps, pausing a moment to watch her, a dream sprite with the moonlight showering down onto her silvery-blond head.

She turned as he approached, saw he had pulled on a pair of jeans, but was bare chested. "Dak, I'm sorry. Did I waken you?"

"No. I was already awake. Thought you might like some company. Besides," he jerked his head toward the castle where Nat King Cole's "Darling, Je Vous Aime Beaucoup" was winging its way through the night air, "no point in wasting good music."

He did not ask, simply took her into his arms, and began to dance. "Mr. Cole's music goes perfectly with moonlight," he murmured in her ear.

She was silent until the end, but before the next song could begin, she peered up at him and said, "He had blue eyes. It was those beautiful blue eyes, looking at me from across the room that I fell in love with." She blinked swiftly, as though trying to curb tears.

After a while, she said thoughtfully, "I don't think he meant to be a rat."

"I'm sure he didn't," Dak agreed politely. "Probably just got caught up in the moment."

"He had the nicest smile," she said wistfully.

"So he was a rat with a nice smile," Dak said jovially and was pleased to see a tiny smile flutter around her mouth.

They fell silent again, dancing slowly to Nat's "Unforgettable" to which Dak couldn't resist humming.

And when she spoke again, she seemed defensive. "It really is over, you know. I think I knew it before I ever saw him, before the memories came flooding back."

He made no reply but did cease humming.

"He thinks he still loves me, but I'm not sure he ever did."

"Oh, I think he did," Dak assured her.

"Maybe at first," she conceded.

"How about you, Goldilocks?" he asked softly.

"I'll be all right."

"No. I mean, do you . . . still love him?"

She shook her head slowly.

"Will you be all right?" he asked. "When you go back to that other life, I mean?"

"Yes," she whispered. "Of course, I will. Besides, no one ever died of a broken heart."

They continued to dance, circling round the courtyard with moonbeams as their overhead lighting. She leaned her head against his bare chest, listening to the steady beating of his heart, and taking comfort from his strength.

When next she spoke, the words were softly muted, and she didn't look up. "It was my fault, you know."

Dak was startled. "What do you mean?"

"Our relationship . . . as you know from this morning . . . wasn't what you would expect from a 90's engaged couple."

"That was your choice," Dak said gently. "You owe no one, including myself, an explanation. Everyone must do what is right for them."

She laughed shortly. "It sounds so simple. But that was the problem. It wasn't his choice. We fought about it a lot. He called it my 'unrealistic whim.' Perhaps, if I had, he would not have -- "

Dak interrupted her words giving her a

little shake. "Don't do this to yourself, Goldilocks!" he demanded, holding her back from him, so he could look down into her face. "Don't apologize. If it seemed the right thing for you, then it probably was. Branson's unfaithfulness was not your fault."

He bent toward her face. "You must believe that," he said softly. "We are each responsible for our own actions. It makes no difference what the circumstances were. He can blame only himself," he finished firmly.

She pushed back into his arms again, nestling her head against his bare chest, where the dark, curly hairs tickled her cheek. There was something she needed to say to him, had to explain, but she kept her head bowed when she said it. "About this morning, Dak. If I had known -- " Her head suddenly jerked up, eager to explain, lest he misunderstand. "I . . . I wasn't just teasing you . . . I honestly didn't know. I really wanted . . . I . . . "

"Don't struggle, Goldilocks," he interrupted. "I know you didn't know. You don't owe me any apologies either."

"But I don't want you to think -- "

Again he interrupted, placing a forefinger over her lips. "I don't think anything," he said, "except that, while I have enjoyed your company, I wish you all the best upon your return to Nashua. Go home," he said softly, "and be happy."

Camilla looked away. Well, what had she expected him to say, anyway? To beg her to stay? She was suddenly conscious that the music had stopped.

"Mr. Cole isn't singing anymore," she said

quietly.

"So he isn't," Dak replied, releasing her. "Perhaps we should call it a night as well? Tomorrow will be a long day. You haven't forgotten the joust tomorrow afternoon?"

She shook her head, and he took her hand as they walked across the bricked courtyard.

15

You know
That if you were for a time in mortal danger,
And are so still . . .

                              Nemerov

*T*he following morning Dak announced over breakfast that he must ride over to the carnival grounds for awhile. "Will you be all right for a few hours?"

"Of course," she waved him away. "Go do whatever you have to do. I'll just amuse myself, maybe take a little walk."

"Don't wander too far," he cautioned.

She smiled. "Don't worry about me, Dak. I can look after myself."

"I just meant that you're not strong yet, you -- "

She shook her head. "I am completely recovered, and I feel just fine. Go tend to your business. I will be all right," she said firmly.

When he looked as if to protest, she said, "I'm not some hothouse flower that you have to hover over, Dak. My father traveled a lot. In spite of the household employees, I learned to take care of myself a long time ago."

His eyes studied her for a long moment. He couldn't help but note the wistfulness in her words. But he didn't comment on it. Instead, he just said, "I'll be back in plenty of time to get ready for the jousting match."

She waved as he strode to the door. When he reached it, he turned back and winked, then pulled it shut behind him.

Camilla strolled leisurely along the beach, soaking up the warm rays of an early spring sun. She slipped her foot out of her shoe and stuck it in the water. It was still cool, and she drew back, the image coming unbidden to her mind of the cool waters of the pool below the cascade in the cave. A smile feathered across her mouth. Palms outward, she shoved her hands into the back pockets of her jeans, strode back up the beach, and climbed the rickety old stairs.

At the top of the iron stairway, she followed the path that led to the cave. Looking up at the dark crevice that signaled the entrance, Camilla smiled again, remembering the wonders that lay beyond. She turned away from the rocky slope that wound upward to the path that led into the wooded area beyond. Assuming it probably intersected the woodland drive, which they had taken when they rode Rajah to the fair, she followed it even though it had become encroached with weeds. A bird squawked overhead, and she paused, shielding her eyes with her hand to watch as it soared across the tree tops. She should have saddled Rajah. It would have been a glorious ride, galloping through the woods, clinging to Rajah as he streaked along racing with the wind, his mane flying wildly, and his tail, a black, arched plume.

A shout broke into her thoughts. More demanding, it came again, and she moved forward to the edge of the forest. When she approached the perimeter of the woods, the rooftop of a house with many chimneys was visible. Camilla was shocked to realize she had come as far as the mansion that overlooked the bay. It appeared even more derelict than the castle, and she was surprised that it was inhabited. Out of curiosity, she edged even closer.

Peering from behind the girth of a huge tree, she saw a large moving van. Three men were unloading large containers and carrying the boxes and cartons to the side of the building where there was an outside entrance. No doubt, the basement of the mansion, she surmised. It was a perfect setting for covert activities. Aware that the movers hardly seemed like your ordinary moving men, her glance flicked over the mansion. It was definitely not ready to move into. Camilla frowned, wondering what they were doing.

Even as the question entered her mind, also streaking across her senses was Dak's primary reason for being at the castle. Could they be storing illegal arms destined for enemy countries in the basement of the old, abandoned house? Her intuition was telling her that it was very likely. She must get back and give the information to Dak. If this were part of the illegal activities he suspected were going on in the area, he would want to relay the information to Casper. Once again, she wished she weren't leaving in the morning, having no doubt it would be interesting to watch Dak in action.

She backed slightly away, intending to retreat. Just as she did so, one of the men turned so that he was facing directly toward her, enabling her to see him quite plainly. Camilla caught her breath, instantly recognizing the man who had knocked her to the ground after Dimitri had been killed. She stood rooted to the spot, staring. Every instinct, punctuated with disquieting little prickles, told her she had stumbled onto something sinister and dangerous.

At the same moment, some inner feeling had obviously prodded the man into sensing he and his companions were being observed. The notion induced him to look up, and when he did, he saw Camilla as plainly as she saw him. Recognition crossed his swarthy features. His feet were suddenly mobilized into action. Before another thought passed through Camilla's mind, she realized the man was running toward her. Immediate fear clutched at her, and wheeling, she ran through the woods, leaping over small limbs and clumps of weeds that obstructed the path.

Once more, she wished she had taken Rajah out for a ride. Outpacing the man behind her would have been a piece of cake. Instead, she raced onward, not daring to look behind her to see if he were gaining. Hearing his heavy footsteps crashing through the woods was enough evidence to prove to her that he was in close pursuit.

Camilla reached the intersection where the path led to the cave above her and the bay beyond. Veering sharply, she struggled up the rocky incline toward the cave. Small stones tumbled down behind her, and while she feared they might lead him to discover where she was, there was no time to be more careful in her assent. She had to find an immediate hiding place.

She reached the crevice in the stone wall that now looked like a haven to her when once it had appeared quite frightening. She ran inside, allowing the gloomy interior to swallow her up in its sepulchral darkness. She paused only long enough to allow her eyes to grow accustomed to the duskiness all around, a duskiness that enveloped her like a cocoon.

Frantically, she searched for a ledge above eye level, or a crevice wide enough to slip into, anything that would serve as a device in which to hide. She moved forward, her hand outstretched on the rough wall, her eyes swinging from side to side. And then her fingers felt the opening. To her left, she saw a horizontal lip that looked as if it were only an overhanging portion of rock, but in the dimness, she could see a slender opening.

Hard foot treads became audible, booted feet scraping on the rocky escarpment, and she knew he was following her into the cave. There was no time to lose; she had to wedge her body into that opening. There was, also, not a second to wonder about -- or fear -- horrid, creepy things that might be lurking within. She turned sideways, forcing her slender figure into the crevice. She felt two buttons on her blouse pop loose as she compressed herself into the slim opening.

Once in, she realized it was comfortably spacious, enabling her to squeeze back out of sight should he also discover the opening. Feeling confident he was too large to push through the opening, she leaned back waiting to see if he would enter the cave.

She did not have long to wait. The man had gained the entrance. His heavy breathing preceded him, and fearfully, she shrank back. Her ears told her he had moved several steps inside the cave, and slowly, she bent forward, and peered out. She saw him standing there, apparently waiting for his eyes to adjust, just as she had done, but then he moved further into the interior. When his searching proved fruitless, he passed by again as he strode to the entrance. Camilla breathed a sigh of relief.

On the threshold of the cave, he turned back, and she saw him looking straight at the stone lip that concealed her hiding place. Her heart nearly stopped. His footsteps carried him there swiftly. The white buttons of her blouse lay on the dirt floor, staring up like pearly eyes, in mute testimony to her hastily sought sanctuary. There was no time to retrieve them.

Camilla shrank back as far as she could go, not daring to breathe. A scream almost bubbled past her terrified lips when she saw his brawny arm thrust through the crevice. Quite plainly, she saw the thick hand with dark hairs curling all over the top, moving around, feeling in the dark void, searching for her. His hand touched the wall directly adjacent, and terrifyingly, his fingertips came within inches of her erect body straining against the cave wall at her back. She closed her eyes, swallowing over a lump, as he withdrew. She stayed where she was, praying he did not wait outside for her to exit, waiting so long, that she became cramped from standing in the small aperture.

She finally decided it was safe to leave, was even more anxious to get out into the fresh air, and back to the safety of the castle. Camilla started to squeeze out of the opening. But something was dreadfully wrong. The opening seemed too small. She tried again. She couldn't get out! Panic spread over her and a claustrophobic crawl began its insidious creep. Dear God! She was stuck! She couldn't get out! She tried again. But there simply wasn't room. She felt like she was suffocating, that the gray rock walls were closing in on her. The rumblings of a scream, racing upward from the pit of her stomach, brought her to her senses.

Slowly, she stifled the terror welling within her small frame, fighting resolutely for self-control. Like one demented, she spoke aloud to herself. "Don't panic, Camilla. Take a deep breath. If you managed to get in, then you have to be able to get out."

Willing herself to take a deep breath, to control her hasty movements, she stepped sideways into the opening once more. Erect, and pulling in every muscle that would move, she eased herself into the crevice. Miraculously, she slipped through like her body had been greased with butter.

Camilla fell to her knees with sheer relief and mental exhaustion. Her breath came in tiny gasps. She rested a moment, her head bowed as she fought to quell the nausea that rose in her throat. And then she saw the pearly buttons lying broken in the dirt, crushed beneath heavy boots, and her narrow escape filled her with fear once more.

At no other time, since she had become aware of the cavernous hole in the side of the cliff, was she more conscious of the cave's fickleness than she was at that moment. It was simultaneously friend and foe, with its beauties, and it dangers, both hidden, intertwined like the twisted fibers of a rope, melding into one curious phenomenon.

Camilla rose on shaky legs, moved cautiously to the opening of the cavern, and peered out. Surely, the man had retreated by now. She prayed he had, for she was not staying here another moment. With that thought barely made known to her consciousness, she ran out of the cave and, slipping and sliding, made her way to the path below. Once, she fell, sliding on her bottom for a good five yards. But she paid it no heed as she regained her footing and continued the race up the path toward the castle.

Thankful to see the castle courtyard in sight, she slowed her frantic pace, wondering if Dak had returned, and offered up another little prayer that he had, for she did not relish the thought of being alone. Approaching the front, she saw that Dak's car was not in the drive, and frowned, eager to relate the details of her harrowing escape, and to seek comfort from his quiet strength.

As she turned the corner, she saw a man peering into the small, leaded pane window set into the oval topped door of the castle. He glanced surreptitiously around him, tried the door, and peered once again through the window.

Thank goodness she had slid the heavy bolt into place before she left. But she had exited the back door, which was not locked. Camilla looked around, panic raising the short hairs at the nape of her neck. She recalled Dak telling her once to run out of the castle and hide in the woods at the slightest hint of trouble. Well, thank you very much for the advice, but after her hide-and-seek game in the cave, be damned if she were going to hide in the woods. She'd had enough fright for one day, she thought querulously, looking around for a likely weapon.

She spied a small clay pot that had once held some kind of flower. The stems were dried a deep brown, and the dirt was as dry as the desert. She lifted it, hoping it was heavy enough to bring the man down. She had never been very good at sports and knew there was no hope of throwing it and having it find its mark. Nor did she intend to wait around for him to gain the upper hand. She saw nothing to do but slip up on him and knock him out. With a satisfied nod for her bold, decisive plan of action, she started stalwartly forward, moving step by measured step.

Slowly, she crept toward the man. Just as he must have heard the light fall of her footsteps, he started to turn. But Camilla sprang forward, like an enraged lion protecting her cub, and brought the clay pot down on his head with a resounding whack. The man crumpled.

Camilla turned away from him for a moment when she heard Dak's car coming into the courtyard. He brought the vehicle to a screeching halt and leaped out, calling her name.

But her frenzied scream drowned out his voice for glancing back down, she saw the stranger starting to stir. She reached for a broken shard of the pot that had broken into several pieces upon impact.

"Dak! Dak!" she yelled. "Hurry! He's getting up again!"

Dak ran up, grabbing her hand that had risen poised to attack the intruder again, though the small piece of pottery was hardly ample to deal another resounding whack.

"Camilla! No! It's Earl!"

She looked up at him, eyes wide and wild.

"It's Casper!" he explained, when he thought she didn't comprehend.

She looked back down at the man in the dark suit that was just a ghost voice to her. "Casper?" she whispered. Then suddenly dropped to her knees. "Oh, my goodness, I'm so sorry." She brushed at his shirt front, with nervous, fluttering hands. "I'm so sorry, Casper. I didn't know it was you. I thought . . . I thought you were . . . "

She rocked back on her heels. "It's all this subterfuge. I don't feel like I'm living in the real world. Everyone seems so suspicious. And now, after seeing that . . . that man . . . and his chasing me . . . "

She stopped and Dak, seeing the quivering lower lip, knew nerves were about to give vent to tears.

"What man?" he asked gently. "Who chased you?"

"Who the hell is Casper?" Earl Babcock demanded.

"You," Dak said aside, paying the man little mind, then repeated his question. "Who chased you, Camilla?"

"The man who killed Dimitri," she said absently, turning her attention to the elder man still sitting on the ground. "Here, Sir, let me help you up. I'm so sorry for hitting you, but I didn't know who you were."

"For heaven's sake, girl, stop apologizing," he demanded, getting to his feet. "It's all right," he said condenscendingly. Then noting the crestfallen features, said jovially, "It's not the first time a woman has clobbered me, though it is the first time one's knocked me off my feet!"

"Come inside," Dak said, skirting a quick

glance over his partner, making sure that he did only suffer a bump to the head. It did amuse him, however, that with all the years experience Earl Babcock had had dodging far deadlier shadows, he had allowed a little slip of a thing like Goldilocks to catch him off guard.

Inside the castle, sitting in chairs set semi-circularly in front of the huge fireplace with the marble gargoyles staring blankly out at them, Dak asked his partner, "What brings you up here?"

"Later," the man said shortly, "let's hear what Goldilocks has to say."

"Mine can wait, if you two want to talk privately," Camilla offered. "I don't mind going to the kitchen or even, by the looks of me, taking a bath."

For the first time, Dak realized she was dirty, her clothing was smudged, she had scrapes on her elbows and was missing two buttons on the front of her blouse.

He pointed, "I think we should hear what has happened to you. You look -- " he waved his hand in a circular motion, searching for a word.

"A wreck?" she supplied for him.

A vague smile crossed his features. "What happened?" he asked.

"I went for a walk just as I told you I was going to do," she began.

Nodding. "And?" he prompted.

"I walked up past the cave to the path just beyond it. Actually," she shrugged, "I wasn't going anywhere in particular. Just a casual walk in the woods. But near the end, I heard a voice shouting; and when I went to look, I saw I had gone as far as that old mansion on the cliff overlooking the bay. You remember, Dak," she said, "the one we saw when we went for a row?"

Again he nodded, but his features were very serious.

"There were three men and a large moving van. They were unloading boxes and seemed to be carrying them into the lower level of the house, probably the basement," she added.

"Could you tell what they were carrying?" Casper asked. "Are you sure it wasn't furniture?"

Camilla shook her head. "It wasn't furniture," she said solemnly. "One of the men looked my way, and I recognized him as the man who knocked me down outside the gypsy fortune teller's tent when Dimitri was killed."

"Are you sure, Camilla?" Dak asked, leaning forward in his chair.

She nodded. "I'm sure. It would be pretty difficult to forget the look on his face as he burst through that tent, especially with a bloody knife in his hand."

"Did he see you?" he asked.

Again she nodded and heard Casper swear.

"He chased me," she said quietly.

Casper and Dak both swore that time.

"I'm sorry," she directed the apology to Dak. "I know I promised not to get in your way."

Dak waved the apology aside. A man's long stride could easily out distance someone of Camilla's slight stature. "How did you get away?" he asked quietly.

"I hid in the cave. In a crevice in the wall. He came in and looked around, but he wasn't sure where I had gone. He was too large to fit through the opening." She peered up at the two men. "But he stuck his hand through, I guess proving to himself that I couldn't have been in there. I nearly stopped breathing when that hairy paw waggled within inches of me."

She paused a minute, fiddling with the front of her blouse where she was minus the two buttons. "I lost these," she explained, "squeezing through." She saw no need to tell them how close she came to being overcome with claustrophobia.

"It's your business," she said, "but I really think they are the ones you're looking for."

Casper's and Dak's eyes met.

"I think she's right," Dak finally said to his partner.

He was surprised to get a nod of agreement. "No doubt about it. We have learned that Dennis -- Dimitri -- was involved in this weapons smuggling deal. We just need the proof." His eyes held Dak's frankly.

"We have it," Dak replied.

His words startled Camilla and Casper, and they looked up sharply.

"What do you mean?" Casper asked.

"All this time I've been watching the water." He shook his head. "Goldilocks just proved what I had begun to suspect."

"What? They're not using the waterways?" his partner asked.

"They are, but they are not receiving by way of the water. The arms are being delivered by trucks and stored in that old abandoned mansion."

"Then how the hell are they getting them out of the country?" Casper demanded.

"There are caves all along this coast. My guess is that there are tunnels leading from the basement of that old house down to the water. A smaller boat could come in and out of that cove virtually unnoticed."

"And the arms transported to a larger vessel somewhere else," Earl finished for him.

"Exactly," Dak nodded.

Casper's bushy eyebrows rose. "Looks like we've got them."

Dak nodded. "When do you want to close in?"

"Let's get you through this damn joust. Next time," he scowled good naturedly, "let's not be so inventive when you need a cover." His head moved complacently, "And, starting immediately, we take turns watching for a boat. If they were unloading a delivery today, chances are we won't have long to wait until the pick up arrives. Any size boat . . . no matter how small or insignificant . . . we investigate it."

"Right." Then, "Aren't you coming to the jousting match?"

Casper shook his head. "No. I'll take first watch." His inclined his head toward Camilla. "You take Goldilocks."

"It isn't necessary that I go," Dak said.

Casper shook his head. "Yes, it is. We've gone to too much trouble setting you up as a potential buyer and resident. No. Not a good idea not to show up. We don't know how long we will have to wait to make our move. I don't think we should jeopardize it by having you withdraw from the competition. We can not afford to create any suspicion."

"Moth," Dak began quietly. "I seriously doubt anything is going to happen in broad daylight. These boys are not stupid. They aren't going to risk loading a boat in the afternoon. I think you should come to the fair with us."

Earl Babcock's brows knitted as he surveyed

146

his friend. He'd known him too long. His motto:
Duty first. Earl frowned. Something was eating at
Dak. Thoughtfully, his eyes flicked over his partner.
Um-huh. So that was it. Goldilocks. He'd seen
Dak's eyes rest momentarily on the girl. Something
damn sure was eating at him. He closed his eyes for
a moment, and his broad chest heaved with a deep
sigh. "You two go get ready," he said. "I'm going
to rest a while."

They had worked together too long for Dak
not to take the proffered cue. He spoke to Camilla.
"You go ahead and get your bath. It won't take me
long to get ready."

When they were alone, Moth demanded,
"What the hell is the matter with you, Brewster?
You've fallen for the girl!"

"It's not that," Dak returned.

Unconvinced and cognizant that he hadn't
denied it, Moth was thinking "the hell it's not!"
But instead, he spoke aloud, "What is it then? Why
are you so insistent I go to the fair?"

"I have this acquaintance, a female," Dak
began.

Moth rolled his eyes. "Surprise, surprise,"
he muttered.

"This is serious," Dak snapped. "This
friend gave me a bit of information, unaware how
important it was to me." Dak paused.

"I'm listening," Moth said.

"Dimitri was staying with the man who
Camilla saw today. His name is Sarnajh. He killed
Dimitri, probably found out he was playing both
sides, feared he would give them away."

"Them? There are others?"

"Rhamsada."

"Who the hell is Rhamsada?"

147

"He is also masquerading as a knight in the jousting match. Calls himself the Black Shadow. He has ties to the gypsy band that has a caravan set up at the fair. I think he is the one with the contacts. He and Sarnajh have known each other many years. Who knows who was the first to become involved in arms smuggling."

"How do you suppose he found Dennis Stanislovi?"

Dak shrugged. "Who knows. Dennis had contacts on both sides of the fence. Which leads me to the reason I need you to go to the joust--"

Moth cocked his head. "What am I missing?"

"Goldilocks," Dak answered softly.

"Holy hell!" Moth blurted, slamming one fist into the palm of his hand. "She's going to need someone watching her."

Dak shook his head affirmatively. "Bingo," he said softly.

"You think this Sarnajh character will show up tonight?"

"I don't know. But he's been there before and if he recognized Camilla this morning, he'll recognize her again. I -- we -- can't take the chance of his getting to her. I'm afraid to leave her alone. After all, he knows she can identify him. He's not going to feel safe with her running around."

Moth was shaking his head in agitation. "I don't like this, Dak. It's dangerous."

"I know. But what can I do about it? We have to give her as much protection as possible."

"Of course." A moment's pause, as Moth's frown deepened. "When is she leaving?"

"Tomorrow morning."

"Good," Moth replied. "We'll keep an eye

on her this afternoon. She'll be all right. But we need to get back here as soon as possible."

"I know," Dak agreed. "The whole affair won't take an hour. We won't stay for the rest of the festivities."

"Good. There is no need to take unnecessary chances. She'll be safe once we get back here." He glanced up at his friend, tell-tale worry lines furrowing his brow. "I'll tell you one thing; I'll breathe a lot easier once she's safely on her way home."

Dak made no reply to that. He tried to ignore the curious little dip his heart made at the mention of Camilla going out of his life forever.

While they waited for Camilla, Dak asked his long time friend, trying to mask his amusement, "Tell me, Moth, how did you manage to let Goldilocks cold-cock you? Let your guard down, old boy?"

"I really didn't think I needed to be on guard here," he replied with a pseudo-sternness. "I thought I was in a friendly camp." He scowled at his friend, daring him to make further remarks.

Dak chuckled. "Come on, old man. Let's go to the fair."

If Camilla were puzzled that Casper was accompanying them after being so adamant about staying, she made no comment about it.

16

. . . we thus drift toward
unparalleled catastrophes.
Einstein

*C*amilla stood beside Earl watching as the jousting match drew down to the two finalists -- Dak, the Dark Knight, and Rhamsada, the Black Shadow. The announcer was telling the spectators that the remaining game of skill, spearing the brass ring, would continue with varied sizes until one of them dropped the ring, thus allowing the other to emerge victoriously. That knight would select the lady of his choice as his Queen for the victory ride around the arena.

Each of the previous contestants had participated in the game of skill that had begun with a brass ring four inches in diameter. The ring had gradually been reduced in size until the present two knights were left, ending in a tie. They were now down to a ring one and a half inches in diameter, a size that would be slowly reduced to a mere one-eighth of an inch, difficult to spear, even for a seasoned jouster. It would be very unusual if the tie were not broken before that, a fact the crowd seemed to be restlessly sensing.

Already the spectators were cheering as the two knights saluted and turned their horses in the direction of the starting line of the eighty-yard track. Three arches rose before them, the first positioned only twenty yards from the starting point with each succeeding arch thirty yards from one another on the straight course. Suspended from each arch was a golden ring. Each contestant, riding his steed at full gallop, must charge through the arches in an eighth-of-a-second time limit and successfully spear the golden ring on his long, steel-tipped lance. Each time a smaller sized ring would be suspended until a winner was determined.

The applause was riotous, and Camilla turned her attention to the Black Shadow. The rider sat erect in the saddle, suddenly sweeping off the red plumed helmet, the only color in his all-black ensemble. The jet black coat of his horse was covered with a blanket embroidered with black silk thread into a glossy design that stood out in bas- relief all around the edge. Rhamsada, the Black Shadow, bowed to the crowd from his mount. His mass of shoulder-length hair was highlighted with tints of copper caught beneath the rays of sunlight. He wore a jupon, a tunic that belted at his waist. In a condescending manner, he replaced his helmet and now sat waiting for Dak to draw level.

More reserved, Dak turned Rajah into place at the beginning of the starting line. Camilla saw his head turn, his eyes seeming to scan the spectators briefly and wondered if he were looking for Casper and herself, or if he were looking for Marielena whom she had seen briefly earlier.

He was handsome, sitting like a prince on the black stallion. Rajah's snow-white hooded blanket contrasted vividly with Dak's black boots and the black turtleneck beneath the jupon. The cascade of frothy white fabric at his throat fluttered in the breeze created by his movements. It whispered of a romantic time long past and successfully captured that mysterious charisma that held the female onlookers spellbound as they watched the two figures engaged in the combat of a Renaissance age.

The final bout was underway as the Black Shadow raced down the runway to the roar of the crowd, successfully spearing the brass ring. The Dark Knight followed suit, and the brass ring was changed again and again.

The tiny quarter-inch circular brass ring was barely discernable in the sunlight as Rhamsada, the Black Shadow, raced through the arches and speared the small circle onto the tip of his lance. He rode round the arena, bowing with a flourish, the red plume on his helmet moving like a live serpent. Turning his mount, he rode with a nonchalant air back to the starting line where Dak waited, observing Rhamsada's performance from Rajah's back.

The crowd seemed to be waiting with breathless suspension for the signal to come for the thrust that may well be the Dark Knight's last ride.

The signal came, and Dak raced down the track, the white plume of his helmet undulating like the back of a dragon as he moved with suppleness beneath Rajah's fast-gaited movements. The stallion's sleek motion was as unhampered as the wind across the plains. Steadily, Dak held the lance, raised slightly in the saddle as he reached the arch and secured the golden circle with a measured thrust of the long spear. He held it without a waver, and the crowd broke into a deafening roar. He rode back to the starting line, cantering very close to the edge of the crowd, acknowledging the cheers with a nod and a wave.

When he drew near where Camilla and Earl stood, he raised up in the saddle and bowed. Then the crowd turned into the direction of a single voice calling Dak's name. They turned as one. All eyes were on the beauteous figure of Marielena, the gypsy dancer.

She wore a sapphire blouse that emphasized the rounded curves of her bosom, and a black skirt so tight and short Camilla wondered how she could possibly sit in it. Her long legs were bare, and her feet were encased in thin, strappy shoes with incredibly high heels that made her legs look even longer. A circle of blossoms was tucked into the black waves of her long hair. She stepped across the invisible boundary of the arena, looking up at Dak. Her breast moved with an upward thrust as she lifted her shoulders provocatively, reaching up to him. He leaned down to her as she spoke, and the crowd seemingly moved as a unit, pressing closer as though to hear. They saw her slender fingers pluck a flower from her hair. She touched it to the carefully painted red lips, her eyes never leaving his watching her through the slit in the helmet. Slowly she offered the blossom to him. His gloved hand reached down, accepting it and the crowd of onlookers, witnessing the seductive scene, went wild, vicariously living the moment. Turning Rajah's head, Dak rode back to take his place.

The final tiny eighth-of-an-inch ring was placed on the last arch. So small was it that it meant picking it off with the mere tip of the lance. The announcer began to chant and the crowd joined in:

> *"The ring is hung, the track is clear,*
> *Charge, Sir Knight, charge!"*

The Black Shadow rode out, and the crowd grew silent, watching spellbound. With measured gallop he drew near. Slowly, he raised his lance, touched the golden ring with the lance tip. It wobbled precariously -- and fell into the dust on the ground.

The crowd groaned, turning their attention to the Dark Knight. Could he break the tie and pluck the tiny ring from its mooring? Or would he drop the ring as well, allowing the joust to remain a tie? They began to chant.

Dak rode out. Camilla strained to see if he had the flower in his breast pocket that Marielena had given him. Her heart was pounding. When he won, he must choose a queen. There was no doubt in her mind that Dak would win. She somehow knew that he would not set out to do something in which he was not absolutely confident that he would come away the victor. That was his nature, a very part of him that she had grown to admire.

Oh, he would win all right. There was, also, no doubt in her mind that he would choose the beautiful gypsy girl. How could she expect otherwise? She would be gone tomorrow, out of his life forever. And the gypsy girl would still be here. She rose suddenly, whispering to Casper that she was going for a cold cola. She had no desire to be witness to his -- no, Marielena's -- victory ride around the arena.

Pushing her way through the crowd, Camilla realized that Casper was right behind her. "Stay and watch," she protested, sure he would want to see his partner win. "I'll be all right," she assured him.

"I'm thirsty, too," he said.

She shrugged, making her way to the concession stand. Just as Camilla raised the cold drink to her lips, she heard the crowd's voice rising cheerfully, and heard Dak's name, the Dark Knight, shouted in triumph.

"He's won," she said softly.

Casper's eyebrows raised, nodding. "He spent some time in England as a young boy. It's been a long time," he shrugged, "but guess you never forget."

Camilla was not surprised at the revelation of Dak's youth. She had been very sure he would not attempt something in which he did not excel.

The voices of the crowd in unison began to chant, "Choose! Choose! Choose!"

Dak rode across the arena. Marielena ran out of the crowd toward him. He bent down to her, gave her a quick hug, spoke gently, and rode on. His eyes scanned the perimeter where he had last seen Camilla and his partner. He removed his helmet, cradling it under his arm. His brow was furrowed as he searched the sea of people. Where had they gone? He rose in the saddle.

Moments later, he spotted her by the refreshment stand looking jaded and alone even though she stood next to Earl. His heart tilted as it always seemed to do when he sensed Camilla's fragile emotions. With a determined hand, he spurred Rajah through the crowd that parted effortlessly, like the sea, allowing him to pass.

The soft clip-clop of Rajah's hooves resounded audibly, and Camilla turned. Her green eyes raised to the tall figure on horseback moving toward them, and she was reminded of the first time she had seen him bearing down on her, looking like a knighted character from a storybook. He rode slowly, his shoulders moving up and down with the stride of the horse. The frothy white lace-edged cravat moved in the air, dancing against his chest in sharp contrast to the black of his outfit. Rajah's footsteps were measured, prancing delicately. Camilla stood mesmerized, watching the scene like a reel revolving in slow motion.

When he reached them, he bent down to her and said quietly, "Come, Goldilocks. Ride with me into the arena."

Camilla held his steady glance for a lengthy interim. His gloved hand reached down to her. She turned to Casper.

"Here," the elder man said jovially, "let me take that." And took the cola from her fingers.

Shifting the helmet to his other hand, Dak bent further forward, put his arm around Camilla's waist, and lifted her up in front of him. Their eyes met and held.

Camilla twisted, drawing away from his eyes. She had the feeling he knew why she had run away from the jousting arena. She took the helmet. "Here, let me hold that," she whispered.

Dak's arms circled around her. Holding the reins, he turned Rajah, and they went back through the crowd to the arena. A riotous cheer went up, gathering momentum as they entered the arena and began the trek around the inside perimeter. Before sufficient time had elapsed to complete the ride, the fickle crowd, just moments ago so enthusiastic, had begun to disperse, turning their attention to the next event.

Dak laughed shortly. "Well, so much for our fifteen minutes in the limelight."

She smiled, leaning back against him as they rode to the side lot where the animals were kept.

"As soon as I tend to Rajah, I'll join you," Dak said, swinging off the horse, and reaching up to lift her to the ground. "Don't linger, Camilla," he said, serious tones masking the casual order. "Go right to Earl. He'll be waiting for you."

She nodded, hesitating. "Dak," she began softly. "I'm glad you won. You looked great out there."

"Thanks, Goldilocks," he said, "I'm glad you were here to share it with me."

They both seemed aware that something was lingering in the atmosphere. Something that they both wished to say, felt the need to discuss, but were leaving inadvertently unspoken. Perhaps neither knew how to approach the problematic situation.

For the moment, Dak chose to sidetrack it. "Go on. Find Earl. I'll join you as quickly as I can."

Camilla stood a moment, watching him lead Rajah away. He turned once, acknowledging her surveilance, inclined his head to her. She smiled, waving her fingertips.

With a great sigh, she turned away, heading back across the lot to the crowds of people on the fairgrounds. She knew she and Dak must talk.

There seemed so much to say before she left in the morning. Would she ever see him again? She hoped so. A life without Dak in it seemed very bleak indeed.

She was suddenly aware of Marielena's flamboyant figure in the distance. Camilla frowned. It was quite obvious that the gypsy girl was heading to the makeshift stables where she knew she would find Dak. In the next instant, a complacent smile flitted across Camilla's mouth. Dak had sought her out despite the open invitation from the gypsy girl.

She stepped lighter, moving to the side of a tent where she stopped to cast a glance around the carnival grounds trying to locate Casper. Her glance roved over the bystanders at the refreshment stand, but she did not see him among them. She frowned, wondering fleetingly in which direction she should head.

Her gaze lingered beyond the outskirts where she stood to a gyrating whirly-gig that spun at such a crazy speed that she could hear the young people screaming even at this distance. Their screams of frenzied delight filled the air, and Camilla couldn't help but think it took a mighty strong constitution to embark on the ride billed as "the thrill of your life." She shook her head in wonderment of such youth-oriented thrills.

A muted movement behind her caused her to look over her shoulder. Her mouth opened to scream, but it was too late. A burly arm gripped her with the strength of a bull. She struggled, but it was to no avail. Panic-stricken, she felt the grip grow tighter and consciousness ebb away like an outgoing tide.

17

*Fear cannot be without hope
nor hope without fear.*
                                    Spinoza

*E*arl strode through the fairgrounds toward
the stables. A deep frown etched his brow. His
sharp gaze swung from side to side. Camilla was
nowhere in sight. An uneasiness gripped him,
hoping, against a prescient fear that was beginning
to engulf him, that she was with Dak. Just as he
reached the outskirts, he saw Dak emerge from the
stable area where he had just put Rajah into a horse
trailer in readiness for the trip back to the castle.
Noting he was alone, Earl's heart sank.

When Dak caught sight of him, he hurried
his gait, calling out, "Where is Camilla?"

Earl shook his head. "I had hoped she was
with you. She didn't come back to the refreshment
stand."

Dak swore, casting a quick look around,

and Earl paused a moment before continuing. "I waited a while then decided I'd better go in search of her, thinking she might have stopped along the way."

"Camilla wouldn't have done that. She understood there might be danger. Besides, I insisted she go right back to where you were, and she agreed."

"I don't like this at all," Earl muttered.

Dak's mouth was set in a grim line.

"Do you think she might have just left?" Earl asked, running his hand over the top of his hair in a frustrated, but thoughtful manner.

"No," Dak shook his head vehemently. "She would not have done that."

Earl's mouth was twisting, mulling over words he hesitated to say. "She seemed uneasy toward the end of the joust," he began.

Dak eyed him sharply. He knew what was bothering Camilla. Some inner sense was telling him she was reluctant about leaving the castle and, he admitted, him. But much as he felt the same unwillingness to see her go, he knew it must be done. She had to go back to that other life, to test it, to see where she belonged. He had no right to ask her to do otherwise, until she knew for herself what she must do and where she belonged. To his friend, he merely repeated, "Camilla wouldn't do that."

"You don't know her that well, Dak," his friend protested gently. "Maybe --"

"No!" Dak interrupted firmly. "She wouldn't leave without saying goodbye." He eyed his partner stalwartly. "I think we're wasting valuable time. We need to be looking for her."

Earl sighed. "All right. Let's go back to the

castle and see if her belongings are there. If they are --" He left the sentence unfinished.

18

Ah, my Beloved, fill the cup that clears
today of past Regrets and future Fears:
Tomorrow! -- Why, Tomorrow
I may be . . .

FitzGerald

*W*hen Camilla regained consciousness, she was on the floor of a van, and her wrists had been tightly bound together. She heard two voices arguing in the front seat. She lay very still, listening.

"I still don't know why you grabbed her," snapped one.

The other one huffed audibly. "You know that she recognized me. It was too big a chance to let her go."

Both voices were in accented English, and Camilla's heart quivered, fearing she knew who her abductors were.

"And now, Sarnajh," demanded the first voice, "what are you going to do with her?"

"I think it is pretty obvious what we must do," came the reply.

His words sent a knowing chill over Camilla as she tried to put that name to the sinister face of the man who had chased her this morning.

"We have our orders," the first voice replied. "We should not have deviated from the plan. You acted too quickly with Dimitri," he accused. "You should have left it to our superiors."

The second man snorted in anger. "This is no time for regrets. We do what we must do. You knew that from the beginning," he snapped.

The mention of Dimitri made her even more sure that she knew her abductors. Silence eschewed. She lay quietly, her heart pounding in fear. Sometime later, she was achingly aware that they had turned off of the main road onto a bumpy dirt road. Every bump drove the metal floor into her hip. She wondered if Dak and Casper were looking for her.

When the vehicle came to a halt, she willed herself to remain silent, feigning unconsciousness. She heard the door open and then felt rough hands pulling on her ankles.

"She still out?"

"Yes," was the short reply, then came a grunt as he lifted her slight figure and slung her, like a sack of grain, over his shoulder.

Camilla tried to peer through slitted eyes to see if the men were who she suspected. While she could not see anything other than the boots of the man who carried her, she did glimpse his companion. It was Rhamsada, the Black Shadow, Dak's opponent in the jousting match. Camilla's hopes sank. There was little doubt that the man who carried her was the dark man who had killed

Dimitri. With a sickening feeling, she realized her chance of surviving was very slim.

Sarnajh, the man who carried her, spoke abruptly to his companion, striding from the weed-encroached walkway to a path that led around the house. She dared not peer around her too openly but saw enough to know that she was at the old mansion that hovered on the crest of the cliff. He carried her down a flight of stairs and through a dark passageway. She heard the squeak of rusted hinges on an iron doorway. The man swung it wide with his free hand, and they strode through the doorway and down another gloomy passageway.

Camilla felt lightheaded from the swaying movement, hanging upside down as she was. Finally, they entered a cave-like room, and the man dumped her down in a corner not caring that her head and shoulder hit the rough floor painfully. Without so much as a backward glance, Sarnajh walked away, leaving her there like a hapless ragdoll tossed aside. She lay immobile, not daring to move, waiting to make sure she was alone.

Slowly, she pushed to an upright position, her hands fell lifelessly into her lap. Her bound wrists were numb from being cramped beneath her body when he had flung her over his shoulder. She tried to wriggle her fingers. The pins and needles jabbed relentlessly, but she continued the movement to restore the blood flow.

She cast a surreptitious look around her. She seemed to be in a cave similar to the one that led to the waterfall. Across from where she sat, the room narrowed, and she pushed awkwardly to her feet to investigate. Slowly, she crept across the dirt floor, casting a wary look at the tunnel that Sarnajh had disappeared into. She prayed she had the strength to keep her wits about her until Dak and Casper could find her. That she was in grave danger was a fact that prodded ominously at every one of her sensibilities.

Her thoughts played havoc with her emotions as she made her way quietly across the cave floor. Leaning against the cold rock wall, she peered into the tunnel. It stretched ahead into the darkness, and she guessed that the tunnel either went to nowhere or to the bay. Obviously, either one held no threat to Sarnajh and Rhamsada. They were obviously confident there was no escape route open to her to leave her as they had done. If it were a dead end, she was lost, and should the tunnel lead down to the water, she was lost as well, for she could hardly swim with her hands bound.

As that thought streaked across her senses, she immediately began to search for something to cut the ropes. She tried rubbing them against the sharp rock wall. While it might take a long time, there was no other means available to her.

With a resolute step, she went back to the corner where Sarnajh had dumped her and probed the wall with outstretched hands. Her eyes had become accustomed to the gloom, and she finally found a sharp, protruding rock surface at just the right height. She sat down, raised her arms, and began the sawing motion against the sharp rock. If one of the men should come back, she was in a position to see if one of them should approach. However, it didn't make much difference, she thought wryly. If they came back before she could get her hands free, they would kill her, which they intended to do anyway if she didn't find a way out of here. Ironically, finding a way out was of no use if she could not free her hands for the inevitable swim to safety.

Some intuition told Camilla these tunnels led to the bay. She recalled Dak saying the smuggled weapons were probably being stored in tunnels beneath the house. The weapons were then transported to a small boat which got them unsuspiciously out of the bay and out to sea where they were able to meet a larger boat in which to off-load their contraband.

She worked diligently at sawing the rope, stopping every now and then to listen for footsteps in the tunnel. And while she sat in the gloomy stillness, her thoughts turned to Dak and her planned departure tomorrow. She suddenly felt the same overwhelming sadness that she had felt in the car just before she had been struck by the falling limb. That familiar awful loneliness. Engulfing her with that same intensity, she tried to push away the miserable feeling of being alone with no one who even knew where she was and with no one who cared about her.

Some tiny part of her heart contradicted her, whispering that Dak cared. Her eyes closed momentarily remembering his gentleness, his kindness, the way she felt when he held her as they danced, the way he kissed her, his concern for her when they had almost made love in the cave. Did he care as much as she did? Camilla's eyes flew wide open. There! You've admitted it, her heart taunted. It's senseless to stand on ceremony when my life's hanging in the balance, she thought crossly.

She wished she had told him how she felt. She wished they had made love. Whatever else happened she would have had that to store in her memories of this incredible week. Yes, it was apparent that Dak cared. But did he *really* care? Her head shook in frustration. She knew the age difference bothered him. Humpt! she sniffed. What was eleven years when it seemed she had only hours -- maybe minutes -- to live? It all seemed so pointless.

A great sigh escaped her. How could she fall so hopelessly in love with someone she had known only a few days? And where the hell was he? she thought querulously, unconsciously dragging herself up from the black pit of despair. He should be here rescuing her. Wasn't that the way it was supposed to work? He'd come charging in on his white horse and save her, and they would live happily ever after.

Yeah, right! Camilla frowned. That was the stuff of fairytales. This was real life and if she were going to get out of here alive, she'd damn well better come up with a scheme to save herself.

Her mouth pursed into a puckering pout, and she shifted abruptly and began to saw viciously at the rope that bound her. Damned if she'd sit here like some helpless ninny and wait for them to come sailing in here to kill her. She was going home tomorrow. She had a life -- even if it was in tatters, rent asunder from the way she had known it. It didn't matter. She was getting the hell out of here! She continued to saw with a ferocity that belied her slight stature.

19

We listened and looked sideways up!
Fear at my heart, as at a cup,
My lifeblood seemed to sip.

Coleridge

*D*ak pushed through the door of the castle without waiting for Earl to catch up with his hasty exit from the car. He strode over to the bed where Camilla had slept and knelt down to peer under it.

He rose, his mouth set grimly. "Her suitcase is still here," he told his partner who waited at the center of the room.

Earl swore, twisting his large frame in frustration with an angry toss of his head. "Dammit!" he uttered. "I always felt uneasy about her being here."

"We have to find her," Dak said evenly.

Earl turned his head, meeting the steely glance of his friend of many years. He nodded. "I know," he said, cognizant of more than Dak perhaps realized. "We'll find her."

"Should we call in the police?" Dak asked.

"How likely do you think it is that this Sarnajh guy grabbed her?"

"Damn likely," Dak responded vehemently. "He'd be my first guess. What about you?"

"From what you told me," Earl agreed with a rapid shake of his head, "I'd say you're right. And therefore, I'd rather not call in the police just yet. Except -- " He paused.

"What?" Dak demanded. "What are you thinking?"

"That we're taking a helluva chance," he answered quietly.

"You think if we try it alone, we may be too late to save her?"

"It may already be too late -- "

"No!"

"Dak!" Earl Babcock's voice rose, grating authoritatively. "You have to prepare yourself for what may be the inevitable."

"No, dammit!" Dak snapped. "I got her into this; I've got to get her out!"

"You didn't get her into it," his friend began.

Dak interrupted him sharply. "Don't patronize me, Moth. I was the one who asked her to wait until after the jousting match. She was preparing to go." He stopped, swallowing hard. "And I stopped her," he said quietly.

Earl ignored Dak's implication. "We have to make a decision," he said. "If we call in the local police, we jeopardize our own operation, one we've worked on for months, and are this close to a successful end." He held up his thumb and forefinger. "However, if we don't, we may be taking a gamble with her life." Moth had laid the choices out bluntly. "What do you want to do?" he asked quietly.

"We can't gamble with her life," Dak whispered. "We just can't." He whirled, turning away from the granite gaze of his partner and running a trembling hand through his dark hair.

Moth could see the sag of Dak's shoulders as he stood there. He had always given one hundred percent to the agency, and now they were asking him to sacrifice something that meant more to him than his own life. He had always given so willingly to his profession. And now they were demanding the proverbial pound of flesh. He waited for his friend to speak.

Slowly, Dak turned back. He held Moth's steady look for a long moment. Finally, he shook his head. "I can't gamble with Goldilock's life," he said. "I love her." He pulled himself up straight, strode toward the door, saying vehemently, "To hell with the illegal arms!"

When he reached the front door, he jerked it open so fiercely it startled Marielena who stood on the portico with knuckles raised ready to knock.

"D - Dak," she stammered.

Surprised to see her there, and struggling to collect his own whirling emotions, Dak murmured, "I'm sorry, Marielena. I . . . we were just going out."

She tried to peer around him into the room. "Where is your friend? The blond?"

That sixth sense every man in secret service possessed kicked in, telling Dak that it was totally out of character for the gypsy girl to be inquiring about Camilla. This was not a casual question to see if he were alone. Marielena knew something. Senses heightened, Dak cocked a questioning eyebrow at her.

She held his look for only a second. Fidgeting, she cast her glance to the stone step. Dak saw her draw a deep breath before she looked up. "We have to talk," she whispered.

"Come inside," Dak said, reaching for her arm to draw her into the room.

Moth came forward.

"This is a friend of mine," he acknowledged. "Earl, this is Marielena, just about the only friend I've made since I came here."

His words were meant to be lighthearted, with a thread of condescension, purposely intended to ingratiate the gypsy girl. Dak held no compunction about his motives. If the girl knew anything about Camilla, he wanted to know it. His gut was telling him she did.

"What do you know about Camilla?" he asked bluntly and to the point.

Dak saw her dark-eyed glance flit over Earl, and he gave her an encouraging nod. "Earl is a friend. We have no secrets."

Marielena sought Dak's attention. "Do you," she asked quietly, "know where Camilla is?"

Her question surprised Dak. He shook his dark head. "She disappeared at the fair."

His words struck Marielena with visible force, and she sank down into a chair. Her head went to her hands. Dense waves of silky black hair fell forward covering them like folds of satin.

Dak knelt to her. "What do you know, Marielena?" he asked softly. "Please, tell me."

She raised her head and looked at him with eyes that held glints of anxiety in their dark depths. "I was crossing the lot in back of the fair grounds going to look for you when I saw Rhamsada getting into a blue van. I started to call out to him, but then I saw Sarnajh come around the side carrying your friend."

"Are you sure it was Camilla?"

She inclined her dark head solemnly. "It was Camilla. He was putting her into the van."

"He was carrying her?" Dak's arms extended emulating the manner.

"Yes. He had her up in his arms. Her head was hanging down. She . . . she. . ." The gypsy girl's words faltered. "She wasn't moving."

"Do you think she was alive?" Dak's lips barely uttered the question.

Marielena shrugged. "I don't know. I was too far away to see."

"Did they know you had seen them?" Dak asked quietly, a new concern rising in him that Marielena might be in danger as well.

She shook her head. "I don't think so." She ran her fingers through the mass of black waves, agitation lacing her words. "I don't know where Rhamsada met Sarnajh or why he would even want to be in his company. It seems that he has been . . . " she struggled for words, "different." Her hands fluttered as though emphasizing her dismay. She sighed heavily. "He just isn't the same since Sarnajh has come back." Her dark eyes looked upward, seeking Dak's. "I don't like Sarnajh. He is evil. Madame Illiana says he has a death cloud over him."

"Marielena?" Dak's voice held an imploring note. "Do you have any idea where they might have gone? Where they might have taken her?"

Slowly, she shook her head.

"Would the gypsies give them sanctuary . . . offer a place to hide?" He had to ask, had to risk alienating her for the information.

This time she shook her head vehemently. "No. If they knew he had harmed her or anyone else, they would not harbor him." She studied Dak for a moment, then said quietly, "You know, the gypsies are not any different than any other people. A few bad ones give us all a bad name."

Dak's hand went immediately to her shoulder, squeezing lightly. "Of course, I know that. I apologize for my insensitivity."

She nodded, accepting his apology in an eloquent manner.

"Are you aware they have rented the old mansion on the bluff?" he asked of her.

She nodded. "Rhamsada did that before Sarnajh came back, but Sarnajh also lives there now."

"Do you think they could have taken Camilla there?"

"Maybe."

The trio was silent for a lengthy moment, then Marielena asked, "What do they want with Camilla?"

"Perhaps she saw something they did not want her to see," Dak replied evenly.

"You mean Dimitri." It was a statement.

"What do you know of that?" Dak asked, a slight surprise edging his words.

"It has been whispered among the gypsies that he was killed by Sarnajh," she answered.

"Do you think he killed him?" Dak asked bluntly.

Marielena shrugged. "He is capable of it."

Dak met his partner's solid gaze but was distracted by the touch of Marielena's hand on his. He turned his attention down to her.

"I am afraid for Rhamsada, Dak," she confided in a quiet voice. "I . . . I think he may be mixed up in something illegal."

"Like what?"

She lifted her shoulders slightly. "I don't know. I can't imagine what he could be mixed up in, but I feel in my heart," she covered her breast with her hand, "it had something to do with Dimitri's being killed."

"Do you think it was Rhamsada who killed Dimitri?" Dak asked.

"No." She shook her dark head. "But I think he knows who did and why."

Again, a look passed between the two men.

In the silence that ensued, Earl came forward from the background where he had relegated himself, allowing Dak to do the questioning. He bent down, kneeling to be eye level with the gypsy girl. "Have you ever been in the old house on the bluff?"

"Yes," she said, nodding.

"Are there tunnels below the basement?"

"Yes. How did you know that?" she whispered in amazement.

"Just a guess," he tossed the awe aside, pressing for the real information that he sought. "Can you reach the water from the tunnels beneath the house?"

Again, she nodded. "Yes. When Rhamsada first rented the place, before Sarnajh came, he took me there to show me how it led to the bay. It was unbelievable," she told them enthusiastically. "Beneath the basement is a maze of tunnels and cave-like rooms. Most of them just come to a dead end, but one of them leads right out to the water."

While Marielena spoke, two minds were

leaping in unison, devising a scheme to get into the mansion. Hopefully, Camilla was still alive, and they could do that before any harm befell her.

With a hurried movement, Dak bent to the gypsy girl. "Marielena, I must ask a favor of you," he began.

"Of course, Dak," she said softly. "You know I would do anything for you."

"I want you to promise me that you will go straight home and that you won't mention this conversation to anyone."

She nodded in consent.

"It is very important," Dak impressed on her. "Camilla's life may depend on your secrecy."

"I will not betray you, Dak," she said firmly, rising to her feet. "I will go now so that you and," she inclined her head toward Earl, "your friend can do whatever is necessary." Without a word, she moved lightly into Dak's arms, resting her head for a moment on his shoulder.

His arms enfolded her gently. "I want you to know I appreciate what you have done," he whispered.

She looked up into his face. A tiny smile settled across the full, sensuous mouth. With a tender, caressing movement, she touched his jaw with her fingertips. "I hope you find her safe," she said, moving away from him and heading to the door.

When she was out of the door, Dak turned back into the room, meeting Earl's eyes.

Wordlessly, they sprang into action.

20

Fixed fate, free will,
foreknowledge absolute,
And found no end,
in wand'ring mazes lost.

Milton

*E*arl grabbed the radio receiver.

"Who are you calling?" Dak asked.

"The office. We need someone to talk to the local authorities in case we need backup. But at the same time, I don't want any interference, unless we call for assistance. Trent will get them to stand by. Maybe we can solve a murder and complete our mission at the same time." He grinned up at his partner. "Nothing I like better than killing two birds with one stone!"

Moments later, he dropped the receiver. "Done," he exclaimed, whirling. "Come on. Let's get up to that house."

"Wait, Moth."

His friend turned back.

"I think you should go up to the house alone," Dak told him, handing him a flashlight. "Take the path through the woods. It's a short cut -- will get you there quicker."

"And you?"

"I'm going up the shore line in that rowboat I found in the outbuilding," he said, tucking a small flashlight in his pocket. "I'll leave the boat in the cove, just in case we need to leave by that route. I'll join you at the wood's edge."

"Good idea. Meet you there," Moth replied as he went out the door.

"Wait for me," Dak called out. " Don't enter the house until I get there."

All he saw was Moth's hand waggling at him from around the corner of the door. Assuming that meant he was assenting to his directive, Dak shook his head and followed him out the door.

Pointing Moth in the direction of the woodland path beyond the cave, Dak headed for the iron staircase behind the castle. Moth had gone loping off up the path at a gait that belied his years. They had been a good team all these years, and Dak held a fervent prayer in his heart that their luck had not run out. He had to save Camilla. He refused to allow himself to think that it was too late. He rowed vigorously, reaching the cove in about fifteen minutes.

He tried to see the entryway from the tunnels beneath the house that Marielena had said led to the water, but a thick stand of shrubbery had grown in wild abandon, concealing it from sight. He guided the small boat into a marshy lee and jumped out, securing it. While not hidden, it was the best he could do. He searched about him for a means to reach the estate from the sandy cove. Beyond him, in a crooked streak, was an old wooden staircase, weatherbeaten and delapidated. Dak frowned. The damn thing was little more than a ladder. He strode toward it, reaching out a hand to give it a shake. It rattled in the stillness, and Dak questioned its stability. His glance roved up the cliffside.

Blowing air through pursed lips, he swung up onto the first rung. It held. With only infinite more trust in it, he place a foot gingerly on the next rung. Much to his amazement, it held as well, and he proceeded up the next, and the next. About midway up the ladder, just as he was beginning to feel confident that he was going to reach the top without pitching headlong to the ground to break his neck, his foot encountered the next rung. It gave way, snapping like a sapling, and Dak swung against the moss-covered cliff like a giant insect. His hands held a death grip on the stair sides as he dangled, trying to regain his footing. Perspiration stood out on his brow as he drew one leg up to reach the next rung. When he felt it beneath his foot, he leaned against the ladder, drawing a ragged breath. Slowly, he began to climb again, moving cautiously up one rung at a time.

Finally, he reached the top and collapsed across the splintery, weather-rotted platform at the top of the cliff. He waited a moment, collecting his wits, searching out his bearings. The old mansion rose to his right. Vaguely, in a stand of trees at the wood's edge, he could see the shadowy form of Moth. He pulled himself to his feet and slipped covertly among the trees to meet him.

Moth turned at his footsteps, gesturing toward the parked blue van. "We were right. She's in there," he said solemnly, referring to the house. In answer to Dak's questioning look, he held up a gold metallic bracelet.

Dak's brows drew together as he reached for the metal trinket. "That's Camilla's."

Moth nodded. "I know. I saw her wearing it."

"I gave it to her as a momento of the fair." He raised clouded blue eyes to his friend. "Where did you find it?"

"Over by the van. No doubt, she lost it when they dragged her out. It's been stepped on."

Dak's fist closed around it as though he could feel something of Camilla, that he could sense that she was still alive.

Moth touched his arm. "Let's go -- "

Gunfire shattered the atmosphere, interrupting his words. A resounding single shot that brought a look of horrified disbelief to Moth's eyes. They both froze where they stood. Dak's features went ghastly white. Moth saw his lips move, mouthing Camilla's name. Dak started forward, but the elder man stepped in front of him, blocking his way. "Wait," he muttered.

Dak tried to push him aside, but Moth shoved at him with his broad chest. "I said wait!"

"For God's sakes, Moth," Dak uttered, "that was probably Camilla -- "

Moth held him firmly. Quietly, he said, "Let me go first."

Dak seemed to crumble, and Moth thought the usually stalwart man he'd known for so many years was going to break down.

"Get a grip, pal," Moth whispered, squeezing his friend's shoulders. He met Dak's look. "Okay?" he asked.

Nodding, Dak drew himself up. "I'm all right," he said firmly, and his partner gave a brief smile that did not ease the cold fear in his heart.

Stealthily, they slipped up to the porch. The house was as silent as a mausoleum. Moth tried the door. It opened beneath his touch. He pushed it wide and stared into the void of a wide entry hall. They entered.

Inside the vast front room of the house they found Rhamsada lying on the floor with a dark red stain spreading across his chest, but he was still alive.

Moth bent to him. "Who has done this?" he asked.

"Sarnajh," the man replied, clutching the gaping wound.

"The girl? Is she here?"

Rhamsada gave a minute nod.

"Alive?" Moth uttered the single word.

Dak felt his heart freeze. The word hung in limbo, just as his life would without her. He watched for one terrifying moment as the gypsy struggled to speak.

"She was," he rasped. "He's . . . going . . . for her . . . now."

"Where is she?"

Rhamsada lay still, his eyes fluttering. Earl Babcock roused him gently, knowing the end was near. "Where . . . is she?" he demanded.

"Basement . . . tunnel," and his head lolled to the side, the dark eyes glazed, unseeing.

With a shake of his head, Moth looked up to Dak, but he was already running through the room in search of the basement door.

Crouched in the corner of the cave-like

room, sawing at the rope against the rough edge of the stone wall, Camilla heard the gunshot. Minutes later, she heard running footsteps coming down the passageway. Some instinct urged her to her feet. The rope, frayed but still intact, bound her wrists. She scurried across the floor like a trapped animal searching for a hiding place. Some horrifying intuition was alerting her senses that they were coming for her.

She ran out into the tunnel that lay beyond the cave room. The footsteps were growing closer, and she looked frantically around for a place to hide. The long narrow passageway offered no refuge, and she continued onward. She stopped once to peer into another cave-like room which held no escape. Running onward, she entered a large room that was stacked with wooden crates.

At the far end of the tunnel, she could see daylight, but the footsteps were growing nearer. There was no time to gain the entrance, and she raced to conceal herself behind the crates. One enormous wooden crate was upended, and the door stood ajar. Inside this crate were smaller boxes of varied sizes. She stepped into it, pulling the door to with both hands. The frayed rope dangled, a grim reminder that she was still helpless even if she were able to gain the exit at the end of the tunnel.

She stood very still, hardly daring to breathe. Through a small crack in the crate, she could see Sarnajh looking around. His features were livid, and he scowled, no doubt, at finding her gone. He moved about some of the crates, then with a curse, headed toward the end of the passageway with a sense of urgency that held no time to search further for her.

Camilla watched him go, then slipped out of

the crate, and followed his running footsteps. She shrank back against the rock wall as he hesitated a moment before running out into the light. Gaining the entrance, she made a dive for a clump of shrubbery beyond the entryway from where she could see his bobbing figure moving ahead in the distance.

From her vantage point, she saw him drop behind a big gray rock that protruded from the hillside like an ill-formed monolith. She wondered what he was doing. What was he waiting for?

More running footsteps were audible, coming from the tunnel. She pressed deeper into the shrubbery, fearing it was Rhamsada. To her amazement, she saw Casper emerge, framed in daylight with the black gaping hole of the tunnel in the background. Against the far wall, she saw the shadowy figure of Dak. They *had* come for her! And her heart smiled.

She looked back to see if Sarnajh had seen them. He had. And dear God, he had his gun raised, ready to shoot. Her heart knocked about in her chest for the weapon was aimed straight at Casper. She had to warn them. But if she called out, Dak may well run into the line of fire in an attempt to push his partner to safety. Suddenly, with no other conscious thought, she leaped out from behind her cover, sprinted the few paces that separated them, and flung herself at Casper. They went down as a shot rang out over their heads. Sarnajh took only a moment to assess the scene before he turned and fled.

In the next instant, Dak was peeling her off Casper and holding her in his arms. "Camilla!"

Casper lumbered to his feet. "Damn female keeps knocking me off my feet!"

And then he caught her up in a bear hug. "Thanks, Goldilocks, but you took a helluva chance," he said, releasing her, then suddenly as though in afterthought, clasped her to him again. "I'm so glad you're all right," he said, his usual gruffness masked by his softly spoken words.

Withdrawing a penknife from his pocket, he cut the final strands of hemp that held her hands together. When he saw the rope burns on her wrists, he clicked his tongue, his eyes meeting Dak's.

"Come on, we have to get out of here," Dak said, grabbing her hand. "I left a boat in the cove."

"There are weapons in there," she said, pointing back to the tunnel. "Lots of them. Just like you thought, Dak."

Casper's eyes met Dak's, and he grinned. "Now if we can just get the hell out of here alive, we've got all the evidence we need."

In the distance, they heard two gun shots. They stopped. Dak's eyes met Casper's. "He found the boat."

Camilla looked from one to the other. "What? What do you mean he found the boat?"

"He sank it," Casper told her.

"It's filling with water as we speak," Dak said, frowning.

"Doesn't matter anyway," Casper said. "We'd be sitting ducks on the water with him out here."

Dak's eyes were scanning the horizon. "We're going to have to take another way out of here."

His glance flowed over Camilla's dress, and he squinched up his mouth, trying to approach the subject delicately. "We need to get up that bank," he told her. "To that cleft between the rocks. Do you think . . . er, would you mind climbing up that bank?"

Camilla's glance flowed up the steep bank. With a shrug, she said spritely, "This is no time for modesty. Let's go."

They started up, grabbing onto, and clinging to any bit of root or outgrowth they could find. Once, Camilla started to slide, unable to get much traction from the soles of her leather sandals. Dak reached out, catching her by the hand, and heard her wince.

When they reached the top, he said, "Your wrist is hurt."

"It will be all right. Just a slight sprain. We'll take care of it later. Right now there are other things more pressing."

"How did that happen?"

She shrugged.

Casper answered for her. "I think she bent it backward when she tackled me." His hand rested on her shoulder, and his eyes held a gentleness that Dak had rarely seen in his partner's face.

"It's all right, really," Camilla assured him. "It doesn't hurt that much."

"We'll get a bandage on it as soon as we get to the castle."

They moved in single file, following Dak's lead, to a cleft nestled between the rocks. The elongated opening yawned darkly at them.

"What is this?" Casper inquired, peering into the inky interior.

"There are many caves all along this stretch," Dak explained. "And not knowing where our friend, Sarnajh, is, I thought we'd better take a less-traveled road. Besides," he grinned, "it's the express route. It enters into the cave above the castle."

"Well, I'll be damned," muttered Casper.

Following behind Dak, Camilla's sandal had picked up a tiny pebble that hurt her foot every time she stepped on it. She paused. "Wait a minute. I've got a stone in my sandal," she told them, bending to unbuckle the shoe.

Behind her, Casper bent as well to give her a supporting hand as she stood on one foot. A shot rang out. The bullet sailed over her head and slammed into the interior wall behind them. Casper instinctively dragged her to the ground, pulling her to cover behind a rock formation.

"It's Sarnajh," Dak whispered. "He's in here." He peered down in the dusk at Camilla. "Are you all right?"

She nodded. "Lucky I had that pebble, or I would be dead." She turned to Casper. "And lucky you're a gentleman, or you would have been hit when I bent."

"How the hell did he get past us without us seeing him?" Casper demanded.

"He didn't have to pass us. He probably entered further up the coastline. As I told you, there are caves all along this stretch of coast."

He peered into the dimness, holding out a splayed hand to keep his companions silent while he listened.

"I don't hear anything, do you?" Casper whispered.

"No. But he's here somewhere. I think we should split up."

"Good idea. Want me to take Goldilocks?"

Dak shook his head. "No. She can stay with me. Get on the other side of the cave and follow the wall. If it branches off, stay to your right."

"Got it." He rose, placing a gentle hand on Camilla's shoulder. "You both be careful."

Like a rabbit, he streaked across the darkened expanse and was swallowed up in the sepulchral void.

Dak reached for Camilla. "Come on. The sooner we get out of here, the better. I don't like knowing something is waiting, ready to pounce, and not knowing from which direction it's coming."

"Frankly," she said dryly, "I never did like things that go bump in the night."

He put his arm around her shoulders, giving her a brief hug. "I have to admit you've been brave, Goldilocks."

"Ha! You don't know the half of it," she tossed back. "First, I was terrified. Then hopeful, thinking you and Casper would come. Then angry when you didn't," she said quietly, peeping up to see how her words affected him. "After that, I fluctuated between fear and anger."

"In such a situation, we're all entitled to fear and anger," he told her.

They were silent for a moment, then she asked softly, "How did you know where to find me?"

"Marielena told us."

"Marielena!" Her surprise echoed in her voice.

"Yes. She saw them put you into the van. Came to the castle to tell us. She wasn't sure whether you were alive or dead."

"I came to in the van, heard them arguing, and pretended to be unconscious."

"Well, their argument must have become full

blown. Rhamsada is dead."

"Dead?"

"Sarnajh shot him. To Rhamsada's credit, he told us where you were being held and that you were alive, but that Sarnajh was going for you. Sarnajh probably saw or heard our approach."

"I heard the gunshot first. Then hasty footsteps that seemed to echo throughout the tunnel. Some instinct, I never knew I possessed, told me there was danger and I'd better find a place to hide." She looked up at Dak. "Isn't it amazing how fine-tuned our instincts are at critical moments? But I guess you know all about that."

"It's how we survive," he replied nonchalantly, catching her hand in his. "Come on. We should meet up with Moth here."

They stepped through a threshold that looked as if it had been carved by nature purposely for a doorway. Camilla looked around in delight. "The waterfall!"

Dak smiled. "Wait 'til Casper sees this."

"Wait 'til Casper sees what?" repeated his partner, stepping through the threshold.

Dak waved an all encompassing hand that held a flashlight.

"Holy hell! What is this?"

"Our private paradise."

"Amazing," Casper breathed, wandering around to inspect it from every angle.

"Better than waterfront property, wouldn't you say?" Dak grinned.

Dak stood at the water's edge, staring into the crystal depth. Camilla had leaned back against the same rock where she had gone to change her clothes. So intent was she on reliving the moment between herself and Dak that she did not hear the muted movement behind her.

In the next second, the danger Dak knew was lurking pounced. Sarnajh grabbed Camilla, holding her with a gun pointed to her head.

Dak heard Camilla's short scream, and turned, starting toward them.

"Don't do anything stupid," Sarnajh demanded, poking the gun into Camilla's golden hair. "It won't bother me a bit to kill her." His words were icy, void of any compassion, and the cold threat strummed a nerve in each of them. "Now, I'm going to leave here," the man said, "and I'm taking her with me. Don't try to follow or I *will* kill her," he intoned emphatically.

Dak had been up against a ruthless killer like this before. He knew he would kill her anyway. The man had nothing to lose. The only question was when? He started forward. Sarnajh saw the movement and raised the gun. It exploded. The bullet grazed Dak's arm. In terror, Camilla screamed his name. Another shot rang out. This time the sound came from Casper's gun where he stood on a rock across from them, surveying the scene. The bullet struck Sarnajh in the shoulder. The gun he held spun out of his hand.

Sarnajh clutched at his shoulder, releasing Camilla in the process. She fell to her knees, looking up at the blood seeping through his spread-out fingers and running in a crimson streak over his hand.

The man wheeled and ran. Casper leaped to the ground, joining Dak in pursuit. Getting to her feet, Camilla stared, too rattled to collect her wits, trying to absorb the fast-paced action. Suddenly, with a little jump, she ran after them like a marathon sprinter.

Sarnajh raced onward, kicking up dirt with his heavy boots as he fled. Dak saw him veer left and knew that direction led to the brink of the cliff.

"Sarnajh! Stop!" he yelled.

But the man lunged onward.

Breathlessly, the trio reached the exit just moments behind Sarnajh. The man tried to slow the momentum of his reckless pace, but he saw the sheer drop of the precipice too late. They stared in horror as Sarnajh plunged over the side, seeming to hover in the air momentarily. His mouth opened in a frenzied scream, and his dark eyes were wild when they met those standing beyond the lip of the cliff in that instant before he plummeted to the deadly sharp rocks rising from the water below. His scream echoed up the vast height, reverberating against the cave walls, touching them all.

Strangely, Dak was reminded of Madame Illiana's prediction of the death cloud that hovered over Sarnajh. It was not, as Marielena had supposed, for someone else, but a death cloud for himself.

21

. . . nor gloom of night keeps them from
accomplishing their appointed courses
with all speed.

Herodotus

At the castle, Casper headed directly to the radio transmitter while Dak offered to look after Camilla's wrists.

She shook her head. "All I want is a bath. It can wait until then." She tossed her head in Casper's direction. "Besides, you have business to take care of." Remembering Dak's arm where he had been grazed with the bullet, she asked about it.

He shrugged off her concern. "Just a scratch. I'll tend to it."

"Sure?"

"Sure," he repeated, waving her on to her bath.

When Camilla returned to the room, Dak

beckoned her to him. "I have some salve I can put on those rope burns," he said softly, so as not to disturb Casper's conversation.

"Thanks," she whispered back. "They do sting a bit."

"How about the wrist? Think we ought to wrap it?"

"Maybe. It's a little sore." She cocked her head in his partner's direction. "Casper having trouble getting through?"

Dak shook his head. "No. The local authorities are on their way out to get the bodies. He's just wrapping up some last minute details."

"Everything worked out for you then?" she asked.

"Yes. Yes, it did."

"Good. I was so afraid I was going to ruin things for you. Especially, after I gave you my word not to get in your way. I'm sorry -- "

Dak hesitated from wrapping the bandage around her sprained wrist and placed his index finger across her lips, interrupting. "You have nothing to apologize for, Goldilocks. I placed you in the position you found yourself by insisting you stay when I knew I had a job to do, and it could be dangerous. I am entirely to blame."

She shook her head. "I agreed to it. Besides, it all worked out."

His eyes held hers. "I have never been so scared when I learned they had abducted you."

She grinned. "Yeah. I was pretty scared myself."

"Oh, by the way," he said, fishing into his pocket. "Here's something that belongs to you." He held up her bracelet.

Camilla reached for it, a smile on her face.

"Where did you find it? I thought it was lost for good."

"Earl found it by the van. It's a little damaged. I'll pick you up another one if you like," he offered.

But she shook her head. "No. It only makes this one more special . . . especially now," she said emphatically.

Dak leaned toward her and started to speak, but they heard Casper set down the radio receiver and turned toward him.

Earl's face was wreathed in a smile. He strode toward Dak, hand extended. Dak reached to grip it firmly.

"Mission accomplished," his partner said quietly.

Dak nodded, clapping his friend on the shoulder.

Earl turned his attention to Camilla. "Wrists okay?"

"Sure," she replied. "A couple of days and they'll be fine."

The man scratched at his head. "Look, Goldilocks," he began. "What you did back there at the tunnel. I . . . I want to thank you for saving my life."

Camilla smiled. "You and Dak came after me," she said softly. "I guess that just evened the score."

The big man stood there looking at her for a moment, then held out his arms. She went into them, returning the embrace. "You're one in a million," he exclaimed.

She patted his back. "The feeling's mutual," she whispered.

Several vehicles came into the courtyard and

Dak said, "The authorities have arrived. What do you say, Moth? Shall we go wrap this up?"

22

The day breaks not: it is my heart,
Because that you and I must part.

Anon.

*L*ate that evening, as she prepared for bed, Camilla opened the cupboard in the big, old-fashioned bathroom. Her gaze fell on the poet shirt hanging from an antique brass hook. She touched it gently with her fingertips. Like a memory stealing softly, her hand wrapped around it, gathering the soft folds into her palm. Swiftly, as though her fingers had a mind of their own, the poet shirt was lifted from the hook. She held it against her naked bosom. A slow smile crossed her mouth, remembering her initial shock when she found that Dak had removed her own wet clothing and dressed her in it.

With a determined air, she put her arms into the long sleeves and buttoned up the front.

The gathered ruffles, edged in tatting, fell over her hands just as they had done before. She hugged the fabric to her body. It was soft and comfortable, and she wanted to wear it one last time. These past few days had been like a lifetime. She wondered what Dak would say when he saw that she wore his shirt. She shrugged. She didn't care if he smiled knowingly. It felt comforting, and she was going to wear it. Flicking a comb through her blond hair, she left the bathroom.

When she entered the main room, Dak looked up. His glance roved over her in a sensual, lingering way, but he made no mention of the poet shirt. However, his eyes held hers for a moment, prompting her to say, "I'll rinse it out in the morning before I leave."

Still, he made no comment. He didn't even nod, just sat there watching her silently. What was he thinking? Camilla pulled away from the possessive surveilance with an effort. She tried to make casual conversation. "Why didn't Casper spend the night?"

"He wanted to get back, get all the loose ends tied up. I'll catch up with him after I get you on your way tomorrow."

Camilla pushed back the covers and climbed into the bed. When she peeped back at Dak, he was still surveying her in that maddeningly silent way.

"What?" she whispered with a perplexed shake of her head. "What are you thinking, Dak?"

"Too much," he replied, rising. His deep sigh reached her across the room.

"What does that mean?" Her words were a soft murmur, and an enigmatic furrow etched her brow.

He didn't answer, and she sat there watching

him pensively. He strode to the old phonograph, selected a record, and laid it on the turntable.

Camilla was not surprised when the deep, rich voice of Nat King Cole filled the room with his "Unforgettable" that was as much a sound as it was a song. She tried unsuccessfully to block the words from her consciousness. Tonight they held a melancholy note that made her want to cry. Already low-spirited, she simply couldn't dwell on them. At the same time, she wondered if hearing Mr. Cole's music in the future would always bring back a flood of memories of Dak and these few days at the castle that seemed to have embraced a lifetime.

Sitting in the bed with knees drawn up and eyes closed as though to hold back the melancholic thoughts that were pressing tears against them, she sensed, rather than heard, Dak by the bedside. Her eyelids blinked open, the lashes fluttering like tiny bird wings, and she looked up. His eyes -- those blue eyes she had known instinctively were different -- held hers. Wordlessly, he reached down, thrusting aside the covers. His strong hand curled around her small one, and he drew her gently to her feet.

Barefooted, she went into his embrace, matching his step and keeping perfect time to the blue notes of Nat's song. The hem of the poet shirt whispered around her thighs, teasing coquettishly as it shifted with their movements.

Dak held her lightly, but firmly. It seemed so natural to lean against him, to rest her head on his shoulder. They swayed to the music, languidly, sensuously. And when the music stopped, he continued to hold her, nuzzling her neck.

Suddenly, he swooped her up in his arms

and carried her to the bed. He laid her down but did not release her. Dak's body covered her upper torso, and he kissed her with a passion that awakened a response in Camilla so vivid, she was shocked at her own reaction. Though wholly wanton, to react in such a stirring manner, her traitorious body seemed unconcerned. It did not care that Dak's hands touched her in secret places, that his lips were driving her wild with their endless trailing over bare skin. Her arms stole around his neck, and she whispered his name.

She might just as well have shouted it or rang a clamorous bell, for it shattered the spell they were weaving around each other like the cocoon of a butterfly's casing. Dak drew back. Her eyes flew open, wide and green -- and hungry.

Dak shook his head. "Not like this," he murmured. "You've waited too long."

"Maybe I've waited for this moment," she answered softly.

Again, he shook his head. "No." He bent forward, resting on one elbow to look into her eyes. His fingers rifled through the strands of blond hair at her temple. He bent further to brush her lips lightly with his own. His words were a groaning murmur. "Do you know how much I want to make love to you?"

She didn't answer. Couldn't answer over the furious pounding of her heart.

He continued in that same deep-throated voice that only added emphasis to his words. "With others it was only a physical thing. But with you . . . it's like a burning desire. I want to kiss you from the top of your head down to your toes. I want to caress every part of you, to feel your naked body next to mine. To savor and to taste it. I want to be as close to you as possible. I want to feel you around me, to hold you, to truly . . . in every sense of the word . . . make love to you."

Camilla swallowed over a gasping catch in her throat. His words had brought on an onslaught of sensation, leaving her with a feeling that he *had* made love to her. She whispered breathlessly, "Why don't you then?"

But he shook his head slowly, measuredly -- and regretfully.

In answer to the questioning look in her eyes, he said, "You have to go back to your former life, with no strings, nothing to pull you away. You need to go back, Camilla, to test that other life, to come to terms with it. Now that the initial feelings of anger and betrayal are passed, you need to face it again. While I have many desires when it comes to you, I have no desire to become an obstacle in your life." He paused a moment. "I don't want to complicate things for you," he said firmly.

A protest sprang to her eyes, her lips. Her entire body arched forward to object. With a great deal of effort, Dak bent to silence the protestation with a light kiss. "You have to help me, Goldilocks," he beseeched gently. "I'm this close," he held up his thumb and forefinger, "to saying the hell with everything and just letting the animal instinct in me take over."

Camilla knew he was striving for a bit of humor to take the edge out of his words. She also knew he was right. After all, she might never see him again after tomorrow, and she wondered if she would have regrets as he seemed to think she might. A niggling little part of her heart made her doubt it. But she raised up to where Dak was sitting and moved into his arms, putting hers around his neck.

"I'm lucky I got whacked on the head in your yard and not some pervert's," she said, a hint of tears threatening her voice. "I don't seem to have much will power," she murmured.

"Hopefully you would, if it had been the pervert," he tossed back jovially.

She laughed. And for a moment, they were silent, just holding each other in a warm and gentle embrace. Then he set her back from him, pushing the covers aside with one hand. "Come on, Goldilocks, time to go to sleep."

It was after midnight. The castle reposed silently in the darkness. Unable to sleep, Camilla spent her last night in the castle tossing and turning. While unafraid to meet the future and return to her old life, she was, however, afraid to say goodbye to the past. The word was so final. And her heart trembled at the thought of never seeing Dak again.

She lay in the stillness, listening for his even breathing. Drifting, like dry leaves caught up in the whirlwind of a vagrant breeze, the sound floated to her across the short expanse, but she knew it was not the rhythmical breaths of the sleeping. He was lying awake, as well. Much as she wanted to call out to him, her prudent side kept her silent.

She drew a heavy sigh that winged its way across the room to Dak, who lay staring in the direction of the bedstead to the right of the slender castle window. A tiny sliver of moon was barely visible. It gave no light to the obscureness within the castle walls. He could make out no form lying in the shadows, but as strongly as he felt her presence, she may just as well have been lying here in the sleeping bag with him.

Though the castle may have slumbered in the disquieting gloom that hung heavy in the air, there was no rest for its occupants. It was a very long night.

When Camilla awoke the next morning, she was startled to find Dak standing beside the bed, looking down on her. A beam of sunlight danced across her features, and she moved to avoid it. Her eyes met Dak's, and she was reminded of the first time she had looked up into his face. She pushed to a sitting position, shoving her fingers through blond hair that was now capped in sunlight. "Good morning," she murmured.

A slight smile tilted the corner of his mouth upward. He nodded. Then suddenly plopped down on the bed beside her. "Camilla -- "

She waited.

He drew a deep breath, shook his head in an agitated movement, and stood up again. There was a false brightness in his voice, "If you hurry and get your shower, you'll be just in time for breakfast." (↖ NO SHOWER THERE!)

He started to move away as she slid her feet to the floor. The poet shirt had become twisted in the night from her restless movements and she straightened it. Her fingers touched the tiny buttons beneath the lace. "I'll be quick," she said with that same false brightness that had touched his words.

Nervously, her fingers clutched the folds of the lacy cravat, and she murmured as she stepped past him. "I'll rinse this out. It will just take a minute."

His hand came out, detaining her. She looked back. "I'd like you to keep the shirt."

Camilla looked at him, eyes wide, feathered brows arched in question.

Dak shrugged. "It never looked as good on me as it does on you."

He must have thought she was going to protest for he touched the lace on her sleeve, his fingers lingering in the folds. "I'd like to think of you sleeping in it," he said softly.

Camilla had to get away. From his touch, his words, his eyes, his voice. She had to maintain some stability, and she couldn't do it if he looked at her like that. She slipped away from his light touch and fled to the old-fashioned bathroom.

The hours slipped away as quickly as a sunset sliding into the horizon. They were standing at the door of the red Corvette.

"Take care of yourself," Dak murmured.

"You, too," she whispered.

He bent to open the door.

Camilla took one step toward it and turned back. What could she say that hadn't already been said? And so, she went into his arms for one final embrace.

He held her, saying softly, "Watch out for falling tree limbs."

She smiled through eyes glistening with unshed tears. She couldn't manage a flippant reply and so gave him an extra squeeze and then climbed into the car.

The door slammed with a jarring note of finality, closing the chapters on yesterday -- and her future. The reflection streaked across her mind mockingly.

He stepped back as she started the motor and pressed the button to bring down the window.

She waved.

He waved.

Slowly, she nosed the car out of the courtyard and into the winding lane.

"Drive carefully, Goldilocks," Dak called out.

She waved through the open window, and then the car disappeared around a bend in the road. She was gone from his sight, and he from hers.

The tears fell freely by the time she reached the spot where the limb had struck her. The spot where Dak had come riding toward her on his black steed. The spot where he had come into her life to change it forever. She stopped the car and sobbed.

After some time, she started the car again. Ironic, she thought. I was crying when I arrived here, and now I'm crying when I leave!

"Cry baby!" she admonished, sniffing, and turned the car onto the main intersection that would take her home.

23

What peaceful hours I once enjoyed!
How sweet their memory still!
But they have left an aching void
The world can never fill.

Cowper

*T*he months dragged by. Camilla had tried to pick up the ropes of business that her father had left dangling, but the more she tried to absorb herself in her work, the more she felt at loose ends. There was a depressing sense of confinement. She became increasingly irritable in the knowledge that her life was at odds with her expectations. She had the overwhelming feeling that she was going in the wrong direction.

When she first arrived home and Branson learned of her return, he had tried to contact her. Finally, she gave in and agreed to meet him, but it had quickly become obvious to them both that their love affair was indeed over. Just weeks ago, she had heard that he had eloped with one of the nurses from his staff. It brought her no pain, no regrets. She wished him no ill will, and hoped he would be happy.

Just when Camilla decided that she must do something about this horrible sense of lethargy that enveloped her, her father's business partner approached her with an offer to buy out her share. It seemed providential and in the next weeks, working closely with an attorney, they reached an agreement.

By the end of summer, the transition had gone into effect, and she was free. However, being free of the responsiblities of the firm only gave her more time to think, more time to remember. Sometimes the memories, that she had felt would be etched in her mind forever, were like a physical pain. They teased and tantalized her, at once beckoning and yet, echoing the futility of going back. As it had crossed her mind a hundred times before, she wondered where Dak was now.

While the bruises on her body and the burns on her wrists, caused by the ropes Sarnajh had tied her with, had long since healed, the pain in her heart seemed never to cease. She went over and over their conversations but could never come up with the reason Dak had let her go. She knew he cared. That much had been obvious, but apparently his love for her had not gone as deeply as her's for him.

She did love him, didn't she? If not, then how to explain this dull ache that lay on her heart like a cold stone? It was a pain that never ceased, a memory that wouldn't die, and a void that refused to be filled. Oh, she loved him all right. There was no other explanation. Dak had said, "Hearts don't forget." Well, if that were true, then she was destined to have this pain in her heart forever, so she'd better learn to live with it.

Sometimes, she sensed his presence on the street so strongly that she would turn, half expecting to see him leaning against a tree trunk and watching her with that fathomless stare that made her heart flutter in reckless anticipation.

Everywhere she went, she fancied she saw him in the movement of a stranger in the distance. Everything reminded her of him. Only yesterday, she had been in a bookstore and passed by a child holding up a new edition of the classic child's fairy tale, *Goldilocks and the Three Bears*. She had fought an instant desire to snatch it from the child's hands, to hug it possessively to her bosom. She wanted to hold it and close her eyes in fervent wishing as though it could in some way, just as any good fairy tale promised, restore Goldilocks to the castle and the handsome prince. She had left the store without making her purchase and harbored a gnawing fear that insanity was pervading upon the stability of her life.

Camilla stood at the window looking down onto the street below. Her fingers fiddled with the bracelet on her wrist. Her gaze fell on the tiny Renaissance figures whose gold plating had long since worn off. A slow smile inched across her mouth. She knew it was just a trinket, a momento not intended to be worn daily. But she couldn't bear to take it off. Her fingers touched the dangling little figures thoughtfully.

And then, like the proverbial light bulb, an idea leaped into her brain with meteoric force. Her hand went to her throat in excitement. It seemed so right, so perfect, she marveled that it had never occurred to her before.

She would buy the castle! Yes! She'd go

back and buy it! Her mind was humming with inspired anticipation. She would restore it to the splendor it had once known but had lacked for so many years. Having made some lucrative investments, she could afford to take off work for a very long time. That would keep her hands busy and her mind occupied. Maybe by the time the project was completed, she would have gotten over this longing that attacked every fibre of her being and not miss Dak so much. A sudden wistful thought cut into her stirring plans. How she wished Dak could know of her plans for restoration. She drew a great sigh.

Camilla shook her blond head, determined to push away the gloomy reminders of something she could not change. She must pack. She wanted to leave first thing in the morning. Humming a tune as she dragged out her suitcase, she stopped midway, realizing she was humming a Nat King Cole song. She chuckled aloud. When had she stopped thinking of him as Natalie's father and allowed him to become the impressive idol with the beautiful, rich voice that had endured long before his daughter had ever been born?

With a smile, she wagged her head. No use fighting this metamorphosis taking control without her permission. It all seemed here to stay, so she might as well get used to the idea. Dak and Nat were going to be a part of her conscious and unconscious thoughts for the rest of her life. Like it or not, she was going to have to learn to live with it. Maybe memories and dreams were all she was ever going to have. With a firm set to her mouth, she decided that was better than no memories or dreams at all.

Pulling open a dresser drawer, she lifted out the freshly laundered poet shirt and placed it in the suitcase. Her fingers lingered on the lace and satiny fabric, softened by the frequent washings. A secret smile played about her lips as she continued her task of packing.

24

And here is my heart which beats
only for you.

Verlaine

*I*t was a perfect end of summer day, and
Camilla was eager to get started. An air of jubilance
hung over the red Corvette as she made her way
up the meandering coast of Maine towards the
little hamlet outside of Portland that hovered over
Casco Bay. She had made up her mind to go
directly to the real estate office and make an offer
on the castle. The idea had not waned overnight. In
fact, she had become so enthusiastic about the
prospect that she had barely slept.

Without any difficulty she found the office
on the main street in Portland and hurried inside,
anxious to finalize a contract.

Upon making her requirements known,
she was told, "I'm sorry, but Claire Castle is no
longer available. However, we have other
properties you may find just as interesting."

Camilla shook her head. "No. I'm not interested in another property. Are you sure," she asked fervently, hoping there had been a mistake, "that this particular property is sold?"

The real estate lady nodded. "Yes. I'm sure. The property has been sold. It had been on the market a very long time."

"Yes, I know," Camilla said, then asked quietly, "Who bought it?"

The woman shook her head. "I don't know," she replied. "One of the other agents sold it just recently, about a week ago, and I haven't heard any details yet about the new owners."

"Owners? A family then?"

The real estate lady shrugged. "Probably. It's a very large house." She paused, observing Camilla's downcast features. "I have another property of a historical nature you may be interested in."

But Camilla shook her head. "No. Thank you." And turned to the door.

Back inside the car, she sat quietly feeling winded from the turn of events. It had never occurred to her that she might be too late to purchase Claire Castle. She felt an overwhelming disappointment to have come so close to something that seemed so right and then to lose it. It seemed a strange twist of fate that after sitting abandoned and neglected for so many years, just waiting for someone to care again, that suddenly there was more than one party interested in the castle. Camilla sighed, wishing she had made this decision just one week sooner.

She backed the car away from the curb and turned north out of town. She didn't care if she did run into the new owners. She'd think up some excuse. She had to go back to the castle, to see it once more. With a determined set of her jaw, she kept the car on the northern course.

Camilla's hands trembled at the wheel as she turned into the winding lane. Her thoughts raced wildly as she passed the spot where the tree limb had struck her, recalling the first time she had seen Dak riding toward her. The rain was streaking in torrents and lightning was producing an eerie light that held him in momentary slow motion, and she remembered thinking that he was a knight out of King Arthur's Court. It was all sort of surreal. Maybe she was still living in a dream world, and now it was time to wake up.

The Corvette nosed around the bend that brought the castle and the courtyard into full view. Camilla's heart fluttered. How she wished she had not been too late to buy it. She stopped the car and slowly got out. There was no other car, no one in sight. It didn't appear that any work had begun on the property, and she had a momentary hope that perhaps the real estate lady had been wrong. But she knew in her heart that it was too soon to expect significant renovations.

Slowly she approached the oval-topped door. Her hand ached to try the knob, but she didn't dare. Looking around outside was one thing. Deliberately snooping inside was quite another. She turned away, stepping off the stone porch, and headed to the courtyard where she had seen the daffodils bending in the early spring breeze.

She stood there, eyes closed, remembering it all, feeling it in her pores, sensing she could hear every word, every sound. Suddenly, her ears picked up the unmistakable velvet tones of Nat's "Unforgettable". Were her senses that strong, or was her imagination playing tricks on her?

She stood very still listening, and unbidden, tears sprang to her eyes. Her heart began a familiar racing, and she turned when she heard a footstep behind her.

Dak stood there, one hand held out to her as though inviting her to dance. With a sob, she ran into his arms. He held her tightly, not moving his feet, but swaying with her as his lips made a path from her temple to her neck and back again to her lips. Nat kept singing in the background.

When she finally found her voice, she said tearfully, "The castle's been sold. I came back to buy it . . . to restore it . . . but I was too late." Unchecked tears flowed down her cheeks.

Then as though propelled by another, more urgent thought, she flung herself into his arms again. "Oh, Dak," she sobbed, "I've missed you so much!"

"I missed you, too, Goldilocks," he murmured.

Her heart thrilled at the name. "You never called, never tried to contact me."

"I couldn't," he said softly.

"Why?"

"I had to let you find yourself. The way you came into my life, I didn't want you to be caught up in some romantic idealism that might be fleeting once you returned to your normal life. I didn't want you to be in love with a storybook moment. And," his voice hesitated only briefly, "I had to make sure you could say goodbye to Branson, that the anger and betrayal you initially felt would not subside. There was a chance the lover's quarrel could be patched up. It wouldn't be the first, you know." He paused, and Camilla broke in.

"It is over with Branson. I think I knew it long before he did. He's married now. Eloped a few weeks ago."

"Are you all right with it?" Dak asked quietly.

"I've been all right with it since I met you," she said softly.

"Good, because I can't share you. I won't settle for half, or even most. I want your entire heart to belong to me. I want all of you," he said emphatically.

She smiled. "And that's the way I want you."

He pulled her to him, kissing her again.

When he released her, she said, "God, Dak. You have no idea how miserable I've been. Sometimes, I felt your presence so strongly it seemed that if I just looked behind me, or across the street, you would be there."

"I was there," he said quietly. To her startled look, he shook his head. "Yes. I was there several times, just to see you from a distance, to make sure you were all right."

"Well, I wasn't all right," she snapped. "I was wretched. Why didn't you make yourself known to me?"

He shook his head. "I told you. I had to let you find yourself, and . . . this damn age thing kept needling me."

"How can you consider age, Dak, when we have so much more going for us?" she whispered.

His eyes held hers. "You don't mind the age difference?" he queried.

She shook her head. "It's not what I think about when I think of you," she replied.

He studied her a moment. "You think we can make this relationship work?"

"All I know," she answered seriously, "is that my heart will not take another goodbye. It felt like it was breaking into little pieces when I drove away from you."

Dak laughed shortly. "Speaking of that. You caused a rift in mine when I saw you stop the car and weep."

"You saw me?"

He nodded. "I followed you out of the lane and watched from behind a tree. I have to tell you, it took all my will power not to run to you and gather you into my arms and beg you not to go."

"I wish you had," she murmured.

Dak kissed the top of her head. "Tough as it was, we had to do it, to be sure."

"And are you sure now?" she whispered, looking up at him.

"Very sure," he said firmly. He drew a deep sigh. "What do you think, Goldilocks? Want to weather this marriage storm with me?"

"Well," she said, biting at her lower lip. "I had hoped for a more romantic proposal than that. We have all the trappings of a fairy tale, you know." She waved a hand, indicating the castle behind them.

Dak's blue eyes had followed her gesture. "Oh," he nodded, comprehending. Then suddenly he swooped her up into his arms, carried her to the stone bench where he deposited her, and then went down on one knee. He lifted her hand in his. "I love you, Camilla, and think I have from the first moment I saw you. I cannot bear the thought of my life without you. Will you, my love, marry me?"

213

She flung herself at him so hard that they both toppled over onto the ground. Tears mingled with her response of, "Yes, yes, yes!"

He rolled her beneath him, and his lips stifled the ensuing words, smothering them in one long, passionate kiss that was filled with the promise of their future.

After a lengthy interim, he raised up, looking down into her face. Lying prostrate on the ground, she stared up at him. They both began to laugh.

"This proposal romantic enough for you?" he asked.

"Highly unconventional," she laughed.

And once again, his kiss stifled the laughter bubbling within.

When he drew her to her feet, she asked, "What do we do now? We should leave. We're trespassing, you know."

"Doesn't matter," he replied.

"It does matter," she said emphatically. "I refuse to spend my honeymoon in jail."

Dak caught her hand, pulling her along with him. "Come here. I want to show you something."

At the back of the castle lay a freshly painted sign. The crenellated board sported the words, *CAMILLA'S CASTLE.*

She looked at him, eyes wide and somewhat wild, afraid to think it might be true. "Did you -- " she began.

He nodded. "I bought the castle. Last week."

"It's really yours?" she breathed incredulously.

"It's really mine," he repeated. "Soon to be ours."

She bent to touch the lettering on the sign

as much to hide the tears of joy as to feel some tangible proof that it was real. She looked up at Dak. "What if I hadn't come back?"

He shrugged, saying solemnly. "It wouldn't have mattered. There would never be anyone else for me. If you didn't return, I'd still have put up the name and taken some satisfaction from the fact that I had restored it just as I imagined you would have done. From that first day," he stated, "when you were so enthusiastic about it becoming a private residence, I thought of it as Camilla's Castle."

She rose and went into his arms. "I had to come back, Dak. Like you once told me, 'Hearts don't forget' and mine was giving me no peace."

His arms brought her tightly up against him, and he whispered into her ear, "This heart hasn't forgotten one moment since the night I found you."

"I love you so much, Dak," she whispered, nestling against him.

"Ummm," he murmured, his breath feathering across her throat, and his lips began making a crooked little path along the porcelain whiteness of her skin.

A dry leaf fell from the tree above them and skittered over the sign, twirling, caught up in a passing breeze, in a happy little dance that echoed from the song in their hearts.